CW00695266

Ken Bruen

hails from the west of Irel
south London. His past includes drunken
brawls in Vietnam, a stretch of four
months in a South American gaol, a PhD
in metaphysics and one of the most
acclaimed début crime novels of the '90s.
He was a finalist for the First Blood
award for Best First Crime Novel of '95
and was a front runner in the *Big Issue's*
'alternative' Booker shortlist.

The
Hackman
Blues

Ken Bruen

BLOODLINES

First Published in Great Britain in 1997 by
The Do-Not Press
PO Box 4215
London SE23 2QD

A Paperback Original

Copyright © 1997 by Ken Bruen
All rights reserved

ISBN 1 899344 22 5

British Library Cataloguing in Publication Data. A catalogue record for
this book is available from the British Library.

All rights reserved. No part of this publication may be reproduced,
transmitted or stored in a retrieval system, in any form or by any means
without the express permission in writing of The Do-Not Press having
first been obtained.

This book is sold on the condition that it shall not, by way of trade or
otherwise, be lent, resold or hired out or otherwise circulated without the
publisher's prior consent in any form of binding or cover other than that
in which it is published and without a similar condition being imposed
on the subsequent purchaser.

Printed and bound in Great Britain by The Guernsey Press Co Ltd.

To Mum and Dad

1

BRADY'S BAD FUCKED

I wrote it on the bedroom wall, in yellow day-glo marker. Nice colour, blended well with the years of nicotine. So, okay. As the Yanks say, I 'fess up, or – closer to home – I put my hand up, guv. I haven't taken my medication for the past week. If I couldn't go a few days without the lithium, I was in deep shit. Thus the wall message. I'd gotten the job ten days earlier and it entailed a whack of pub crawling. Booze and medication is the worst of songs. Sing that!

A job of pure simplicity. Find a white girl in Brixton. Piece of cake. What I should have done is doubled my medication and lit a candle to Saint Jude – maybe a lotta candles.

Jack Dunphy is in the building game. To hear some of them tell it, he is the game. Leastways he used to be, all over south-east London. What's known as a 'plastic paddy'. Third or fourth generation down the pike and as English as toast. But could shovel the brogue as the occasion demanded. A flash git too. Liked to show he'd the dosh. Word was, he'd married a game-show hostess and hit the top of some minor B list. A name among the 'could-'ave-beens'.

Hard bastard. Odd stories surfaced of punters getting done with baseball bats and the blow-torch. Anyway, not a fella to fuck with. I knew him for years on a vague basis. The, 'How you doing?' dance. Bags of brief enthusiasm and no follow-up. If you never met again, how much would you be hurting? Like that.

So, I was a little surprised when he offered to buy me a drink. The local bookie got married and there was a knees-up in the backroom of the Greyhound. My sometimes pub next to the Oval tube station. I was standing at the bar while a karaoke merchant mutilated 'That Loving Feeling'.

'Paul, whatcha drinking?'

Yeah, he gave it the best south-east London twist. To put me at ease?

'I'm all right.'

'Go on then, 'ave somefin'. Yo' barkeep, couple of double scotches before Tuesday.'

I gave him the full look. He was the spit of Henry Cooper, but Our Henry with a bad drop. Dressed in a good suit, hand-made shoes, and washed to a sheen. No electric razors or Bic disposables for this guy. It was the barber's chair and an open razor job, then the face hand-massaged to a rosy hue. He'd tip good too, ask about yer missus and frame yer balls if you crossed him. A villain with communication skills.

The drinks came and he nodded, picked one up, indicated I should do likewise. I did but put it down, untasted, and he said:

'Cheers Paul. Best of British, eh?'

'It's not Paul.'

'What?'

'My name – it's not Paul.'

That threw him. He was a man who prided himself on information. But he rallied.

'Shit I'm sorry, could have sworn…'

I had some scotch, it tasted okay, like hope.

He put out his hand.

'Let's start over, I'm Jack Dunphy.'

The thought flashed, Who gives a flying fuck? but I let it slide. I was taking my pills. I was mellow and I shook his hand. The grip was solid, let you know he was a man of integrity. You get one of those 'tight with sincerity' shakes, watch your wallet. I didn't have any more of the scotch.

'It's Tony… but most people call me Brady.'

He reached for the lighter touch:

'But what do your friends call you… eh…? Call you Tone?'

'No.'

A silence for a bit, not a problem for me, then:

'Look Tony, I'll be upfront here…'

Watch that wallet.

'I've been told you're dependable and… that you could help me.'

I reached for the lighter touch too, said:

'It depends.'

Took a moment, then he laughed… badly. A laugh a long way from his eyes.

'Oh I get it, yes – very droll. The thing is Tone… Tony, I need to find a woman.'

I ran the gamut of replies:

(1) What, you think I'm a pimp?

(2) The game-show run out of juice? or,

(3) Join a lonely hearts club.

Wittily enough, I opted for, 'What?'

'My daughter, she's gone missing.'

'Did you contact the Old Bill?'

He gave me a look reeking in 'Do us a bloody favour', and said, 'It's not a police thing. Those fucks couldn't find peace.'

I wasn't sure what to think, said, 'I'm not sure what to think.'

'She's twenty, she's my only child. I think she's in Brixton. She was up at Cambridge reading English and just dropped out. I need someone discreet to find her. Rosie, the missus, is going frantic.'

'I'll need a photo, some personal details.'

He took a large manila envelope from his jacket, laid it on the bar, said:

'It's there… and cash… you need more, you call me… anytime.'

The package looked thick, fat with readies, I guessed. No cheques with this outfit.

He nodded at my drink, asked, 'You don't like whisky?'

'Oh I like whisky, I just don't like that one… barkeep, give us a couple of Jack Daniels Old Number 7.'

The bar-guy was well pissed at having to locate this, did a production outa finding the bottle. I couldn't have given a toss. Finally, the drinks appeared.

Jack said, 'Expensive tastes, I see.'

I tapped the envelope with one finger, said, 'Reckon I can afford it. Cheers.'

We drank. He knocked it back. A moment, then his eyes watered and he gripped the bar, croaked: 'Jay-sus!'

'Tennessee drinking whisky, burns like a bastard, you got to sip it… see?' I sipped and gave a tight smile. He wasn't pleased.

'You could have said.'

'C'mon Jack, are you a man to be told what to do?'

'Bear that in mind, you and me will get along.'

A woman had replaced the karaoke and was doing a passable rendition of 'If It's The Last Thing I Do.' Sounded like Tammy Wynette via Peckham. Close to home.

Jack asked, 'You're thinking I look like someone, right? People are always noticing the resemblance… go on… have a shot.'

Could I say Henry… ? I figured not. Said, 'Erm… It's on the tip of my tongue…'

He was like a child with a secret, could wait no longer.

'I'll give you a hint… *Bite The Bullet.*'

Yeah… a horse's ass, but lied: 'Erm … missed that one.'

'Gene Hackman!'

'What?'

'When I give that tight little smile, when I'm fucked about… see… ?'

Oh God, he gave me a demonstration. It was horrible, truly fucking horrible. I had to blame the Jack Daniels… had to…

He asked, 'Want me to do it again?'

'No… it's uncanny… quite unbelievable, you've a real talent there.'

Just then I caught the eye of a young guy across the bar. Long blonde hair, T-shirt, the requisite 501s… he smiled.

I said, 'Gotta go… I'll be in touch.'

He put out his hand, gave me another of those manly grips. Gripped me solidly for a time. He said: 'I think I'll have some more of that Tennessee… do you think?'

'You do that… oh… and Gene…'
He loved it.
'Yeah?'
'Sip it… okay … nice and slow.'
When I got the young guy back to my place, that's exactly how I took him.

2

Next morning I opened my eyes to see the guy preening in front of the wardrobe mirror. Dressed only in white Y-fronts, he was rivetted by his image. A lot to be held by. His body was lean and muscular, of the gym-smoothed variety. Sun-beds featured too, as he'd a light tan all over. My own body looked a wreck.

Catching my eye, he winked and asked, 'See something you like?'

'One of us does.'

This got the blank look and, 'What?'

I got outa bed and yeah, wouldn't you know, my joints creaked loudly.

The guy moved his hands along his chest, asked, 'Would you like a little wake-me-up?'

'I'd like two things.'

He gave me a practiced sensual look, ran his tongue across his top teeth. Rough beginning to a day, rough trade indeed. He near whispered, 'Anything… any amount.'

'Coffee and your ass outa here.'

He got dressed as I made the coffee. I'd run outa whitener so it was black and bitter – like Brixton, according to the Metropolitan Police.

I prised a tenner out of my wallet and the guy said, 'I need a hug.'

'Here's cab fare – hug the driver.'

As he left, he paused for an exit line:

'You're not as tough as you think.'

'You got that right.'

'Call me?'

'First opportunity.'

'Goodbye then.'

'Good something…' and as the door closed, I added, 'riddance', but not with much intent.

You ever hear of Grace Maria Kennedy? Not one of your better known poets. She belongs to the Ann Sexton school of mania. I had her collected poems and, I dunno, they give me such comfort. Or, to grab the current idiom – identification. Fuck it, I just like them. I took down the volume, lip mouthed some lines from 'Levels':

> Ending school at seventeen
> as I was then a
> gutter'd level was
> what they foresaw for me
> I half elated
> on some reputation tough
> as I believed
> believed thru years astray
> should manic give me
> A level
> lower.

The key words always leapt – elation – mania. The words of my existence. I saw a tele-movie called *Nest Of Spies* and, as everything disintegrates, Powers Booth shouts at his wife: 'Keep taking the crazy pills and shut the fuck up.'

As the coffee lined my gut, I thought, I'm the wrong call of fifty, gay, and manic depressive, and said aloud in Gene Hackman voice, 'Jeez, my goddam cup overfloweth.'

I turned on the radio, turned it on loud. Juice Newton belting out 'Angel of The Morning' and wow, what a name. You're bopping down the street and the brothers go: 'Yo', Juice!' Yeah.

I was getting manic. Always happens when I drink, it's like it neutralises the medication. So I brewed some more caffeine and got that lithium down.

Up/down the jangled dance… who wins?

I put the poems aside. Let it rest on Larry Kramer's 'Faggots.' Seemed appropriate, if not important. Few years back, I came across a piece of graffiti, it read: 'My mother made me a homosexual.' Underneath, in brackets, was written, 'If I send her the wool, will she make me one too?' Time to open the envelope. And the Oscar goes to…

The wad of money came out first. Neatly banded in large denominations. I figured the building game wasn't in crisis, after all. Then a six-by-four full face photograph. My first instinct was – Jeez, what a dog! Allowing this was a studio portrait, with all the help of lights and a professional photographer, God only knew how ugly she really was. Straight, dark hair, bad eyes. They had that lidded look of the very drunk or of a lazy reptile. A snub nose and a thin mouth. She looked about eighteen. On the back were the details

Name: Rosaleen/Roz – Born: 3rd January, 1975 – Eyes: Brown – Hair: brunette – Height: 5-feet, 2-inches – Weight: 100 lbs – Friends: Alison Kee (phone number and address) – Distinguishing Marks: Tattoo of small bird on left inside wrist.

Reminded me of a memorial card and I hoped it wasn't ominous. It saddened me that such a young girl had only one friend. I tried to shrug it off, saying, 'What's it to me, I couldn't give a rat's ass if she was little Miss Popularity.' I'd only to find her, not sort her.

Had a shower and towelled off in front of the wardrobe mirror. I skipped the preening but had a sneak analysis. If I stood up real straight I managed five-feet-eleven. My torso had a beat-up effect which was the result of being beat up… often. I did rigorous stomach exercises daily but it hadn't kept a growing pot belly at bay. Shit, I'm fifty-two – who gets a washboard effect after fifty? Maybe I'd get that gut suction job like Kenny Rogers. Yeah… and maybe get lucky too. Dream on.

I was carrying weight all right and not just in my attitude. But some of it still came in as muscle. My hair was fucked, gone and missed. Not that I was bald but getting there way too fast. A broken nose and a mediocre mouth. But hey… I got good eyes. Wide, blue and understanding. Leastways the guy last night said and that was before I gave him cab fare. Some guys, their faces look lived-in, gives a hint of character and experience. Mine…? Naw, it was squatted in for more years than the landlord cares to admit. Did you ever see *A Perfect World*? Clint Eastwood, Kevin Costner and directed by ol' Clint. Kevin Costner says to a kid, 'We got a lot in common. We both love RC cola, both got pappas not worth a damn, and we're handsome devils.' I said this to Roz's photo and smiled a little. It was truer than I knew.

Maybe the job could be done by phone, she could be holed up with her one friend. So I rang her. It was picked up fast.

'Hello… is that Alison?'

'Y-es.'

'Oh good. Hi Alison… I'm trying to locate Roz.'

'Fuck off.'

'Was it something I said?' I asked the empty receiver.

3

Elias Rasheed Mohammed. That was his name during the Muslim phase. I called him Reed. We met in Wormwood Scrubs.

Before the lithium worked its magic, I was on and off a sundry of medication. Few worked. I got two years for GBH and had been sent to the Scrubs. Back in the glory days of two-man cells. The screw sniggered as he pushed me in.

'You get to bunk down with the Holy Man, Brady.'

'Holy?'

'Yeah – like Holy Terror.'

And he gave a guffaw. Not an easy thing but pig ignorance helps. One bunk was neatly made, all squared away with a book resting on the pillow. I picked it up – The Koran – and slung it. Madness was dancing in hot white waves across my brain. Cookin' mania.

I lay on that bunk. A while later a black man showed. Near six-foot-two, he appeared to glow, due to the sheen of his skin and shaved head. Built for endurance.

He said, very quietly, 'Get yer ass off my bed, whitey.'

Two seconds to leap from the bed and smash into him. Then I rammed his skull against the bars and ended with a power-driver to his chin. Out cold. I stood over him and fought not to stomp his face. Moving back against the door, I braced there, my leg ready to level his head. When he came to, he shook his head to clear the vision, propped up on one elbow, looked at me, said, 'There's more where that came from.'

It hung there for a few moments, then we started to laugh. We've been friends since. Way to guess, else I'd have killed him.

He fought my corner for the time it took to build my rep'. Not that it took long – my mania was in full roar. Cons are especially wary of a madman. In a world of random, casual violence, unpredictability is fearsome.

Those years, Reed helped me channel the ferocity and to utilise it. He was a car thief, doing five years.

'Yo' baby… I drool for a set of wheels.'

For a few months I listened to his black power rap then one day snapped.

'Reed, give it a bloody rest! You probably grew up in Maidstone. I was born and reared in Brixton.'

'Don't dis me, mon.'

'Dis you! For fuck's sake will you listen to him. Sidney Poitier has more street cred.'

He leant over to his small collection of books. Selected one and ran his hand reverently along the cover. Then solemnly offered it. Like some priest of blackness. I snatched it. Elridge Cleaver – 'Soul On Ice'.

'What's this shite?'

He sighed. A thing he got to do often, said, 'Man, we gots to get you cool.'

I slung it.

'Bollocks! My soul's been on fire since I was five-years-old.'

Come the first Christmas he gave me another book, said, 'Complements of the season, the white one.'

I gave him the usual – grief. This time the book he gave me was James Baldwin – 'Go tell it on the Mountain' – and he said quickly, 'Yo', don't throw it – you and that dude got something in common.'

'What, he's unhinged – sorta has black depression?'

'No, he be homosexual.'

I was on my feet ready to bounce him.

'You have a problem with that, Reed?'

'No, sir. You's the one has the attitude.'

'Have I bothered you… do you feel threatened?'

He gave a rich laugh, 'Threatened… by you… shit bro'? All the time but not sexually. Wha's the matter with you boy, yo' all don't want my black ass.'

'Yeah, cos you're an ugly bastard.'

Easter he gave me the jail journal of Jean Genet. After I finished, I said, 'That guy's a bloody pervert.'

'Whatcha expect mon? He's white.'

A batch of skinheads were banged on to our tier. At night you could hear them chanting Millwall anthems and mispronouncing obscenities. I'd pass their cells and see them tattooing swastikas on to bald skulls, the bloodier the better.

I had one of them in the mail-room. A sweet-cheeked lad of barely eighteen. After he'd blown me, he asked, 'Wotcha mates with a nigger for?'

What teeth he had, I knocked out.

They began to shout British Movement slogans and bait the non-white inmates. National socialism nor any other political conviction had nothing to do with it. They liked the hatred, thrived on intimidation.

One afternoon they tried to castrate Reed in the showers. The knives just weren't sharp enough. Even in that, they literally couldn't cut it. But they hurt him sufficiently that he was given early release.

I was allowed to see him in the hospital. What a bloody mess. His face was a ruin, both arms were broken, and he was to lose one eye.

He said, 'You should see the other guy.'

'Yeah.'

'It's nothing, just a scratch.'

'Makes you better looking.'

'Roll us a smoke, Brady.'

I glanced round at the mega no smoking signs and he gave the habitual sigh.

'What they gonna do mon – jail my black ass?'

I put the roll-up between his lips and he took a deep drag.

Then a fit of coughing, said, 'They've got a point, these suckers are bad for you.'

I didn't answer. Then he said, 'Let it go, bro' – you hear me?'

Reed had just finished John de Vecchio's book on Vietnam – 'The Thirteenth Valley.' Read it mainly because the guy ended up in prison. In 'Nam, they had a catch-phrase to deal with the horror. Reed said it now:

'It don't mean nothing, drive on.'

'Like fuck.'

'Don't dis me, bro'. I be serious now. Yo'all go after them trainee nazis, yo' gonna get your sorry ass killed.'

'We'll see.'

He extended his fingers and said, 'Touch me, bro'.'

'Get outa here.'

'Please man…'

I did and he tightened that fragile hold, asked, 'Promise me Brady – gimme yo' word, mon. Y'all stay away from those muthas.'

'I promise.

'O-kay… when yo' get released, I be waiting, yo' hear… in a new set of wheels… take yo' to de moon.'

'I've been there.'

'Not with me yo' ain't. Yo' keep that bond… yeah?'

'Sure.'

Dream on.

The prison shrink had said to me: 'Manic depression isn't a complete blanket term. What works for one person may not help another. Numerous other factors have to be clued in. You have a marked pathological aspect to your condition.'

As I was serving time for GBH, how clued in was he? He'd given me some medication – that definitely helped. When a boxer prepares for a bout, he does road work, sparring, weights. Like that. Me, I stopped the medication.

The three who'd done Reed, I called Larry, Mo, and Curly Joe. For obvious reasons. Larry was the one I'd had sex with and he worked in the mail-room (no pun intended). I gave him a nod and he followed me out to the toilets.

I said, 'Lemme have you.'

His fear gave way to surprise, asked, 'Yer not bovvered cos of the nig-nog?'

'Naw… fuck him.'

And I laughed. He gave a less hearty one, said, 'It'll cost you… carton this time…'

'No sweat – you're worth it.'

'Cos I'm not bent like, know what I mean?'

'Course I do, you're a straight arrow.'

He was nervous again, asked, 'D'ya want me to take me dick out?'

'Naw, I'll take it out…'

And I shot my left hand round his throat, levitated him a few inches, then jammed him against the tiles, reached for the knife, said, 'Two items to note, Larry. Firstly, this blade is sharpened. Second, sopranos don't do good in the British Movement.'

Mo was working in the kitchens, stirring a huge pot.

I said, 'What's cookin?'

'Wotcher doing in 'ere – not supposed to be 'ere – is it cos of the wog?'

I looked towards the pot, asked, 'What's that then?'

'Stew.'

'Lots of veggies?'

'You what?'

I grabbed him by the two ears, up-ended him and dunked him right in it, said, 'And here's the turnip.'

Curly Joe I did the worst thing of all to. I let him think about it. A week later, he jumped off D-wing.

What happened after is what happens ninety-percent of the time in prison.

Nothing.

But I'd got my rep'.

4

On my release, Reed was waiting. In a white stretch-limo. Was I glad? Jeez I was mortified. He even had a chauffeur's uniform. Right down to the peak cap.

Said, 'Your car m'lud.'

'Pimp-mobile, more like.'

'Cost an eye and a leg.'

I didn't want to stare, to look directly and he said, 'You can look – see it's not so bad.'

'I can pop the sucker out, let yo' all have a close up.'

I felt ill. He said, 'Let's haul ass before those muthas change their mind. Get in the back.'

I did. There was enough room for a small Third World family and a fully-stocked bar. Reed put the car in gear and we slid smoothly away. Jackson Browne was on the speakers.

Reed said, 'I gots to have dis baby back in an hour, so enjoy.'

I didn't say anything and he continued, 'See how it works… A dude gets released, he has priorities – get laid, get wasted, like that. But yo' all is a different drummer.'

'Cos I'm gay?'

'Cos you a crazy fuck. See the envelope on the seat?'

'Yeah, so what?'

'It's mullah bro', cash money. We be working dudes now but I gots to axe yo' a question, okay?'

'What, you'll want a reference?'

'Lighten up Brady, yo' all a free bird now. I gots to know… did you mess with dem skins?'

'Didn't I give you my word – didn't I do that?'

'Yeah… right.'

My phone rang, pulling me back to the present.

'Yeah.'

'Brady… it's Jack.'

''Lo Jack.'

'Any progress?'

'Since I saw you last night?'

'Oh right – I'm anxious is all. You can't imagine what that little girl means to me.'

'I'll find her.'

'Course you will. The only important thing is blood, family… all the rest are strangers.'

'You what?'

'Gene said that in Wyatt Earp…'

'Did he now?'

'It's the absolute truth.'

'Well, if Gene said so…'

'I'm going to give you something.'

'Not a good thrashing, I hope?'

'A baseball cap… he always wears one.'

'Jeez, what can I say – we'll be two Genes.'

'Two what?'

Too bloody much, but I said, 'I'll call as soon as I get something, okay Jack?'

'You do that.'

And he rang off.

Was it me, or did that sound like an order? Said aloud: 'Never no mind, probably a Hackman thing…' Yeah, that was it. You could tire of Gene though. No doubt about it, he could definitely get on your fucking nerves.

Reed and I had a partnership. Nothing on paper. No contract, no set deal, but fixed as fate. He had little cards printed:

MONEY
PROPERTY
PRESTIGE

Lost anything connected to life's essentials?
CALL US – IT'S FOUND

The cards he'd stolen but I think he paid for the printing. When he told me the scheme, or scam, I laughed out loud, said, 'Bollocks.'

We were never out of work. Go figure. Okay, sometimes we gave it a nudge and stole the item first.

A Labour parliamentary candidate went public on the loss of her beloved Yorkshire terrier. I found it and got a write-up in the *South London Press*:

ACE VENTURA OF VAUXHALL

Even had my photo. Made me look like Ken Livingstone on speed. From his London Council era… Yeah, that bad.

If you watch videos, you know about FACT. You may not want to but you can't escape the fuckers. Slammed in at the beginning of every video – you can't avoid them, like muggers in Stockwell. The Federation to stop video piracy. We did a bit of work for them. A nice little earner and reliable. To cover both ends of the market, we made the pirates… then shopped 'em. A version of Tory innovation. Reed said it was our tribute to the Thatcher years – and cars. Oh yeah, heavens-to-betsy, it's where the gold is. Steal 'em and find 'em… fast. No repo could match our record for instant recovery. Recently, the mountain bikes had become a market mover. Those suckers trade for serious earners. You get a set-up like that, money leaking in from all angles, it's sweet as a nut. But… you're also gonna get attention. Blood in the water and the sharks come cruising.

You get: (1) Scavengers
              (2) Predators, and
              (3) Policemen.

Things were just falling into place when my doorbell rang

one morning. Two suits, one burly and one creepy. Numero Uno began, 'Good morning, sir – I'm Chief Inspector Nolan.'

'And how are the sisters?'

'What?'

'Nothing.'

'If I might continue? My colleague here, though shy, is Sergeant James and you, sir are...'

He consulted his notebook, stepped back to check the house number, the usual bullshit, then exclaimed, '... Mr T Brady. Am I correct?'

'What, like politically correct?'

'Ah, a comedian. How jolly. Me and my sergeant likes a good laugh.'

Then the tone changed. 'Might we step in, sir?'

I moved aside. Nolan went ahead but James hung back, keeping me in the middle. Like in the cadets manual. It was a hot read in prison, the cons loved it. We trooped into the living room. Nolan put out his hand... then the other, said:

'If I'm right the kitchen is that way. Might Sergeant James do us a brew and one for you, of course. Thing is, we skimped on breakfast, keen to make yer acquaintance and all that.'

I said nothing.

James headed for the kitchen.

Nolan flopped into an armchair, took a look 'round.

'Fairly spartan, eh? Is that the minimal effect like them Japs are so keen on, or are you just a cheap bastard?'

Was there an answer to this, short of a kick to the side of the head? James returned with a tray and tea stuff, said:

'Nowt to eat Guv, except for marietta biscuits.'

'What, no bacon sarnies...? Well, pour the tea, we can't very well expect our Mr Brady to attend to us hand and foot.'

James continued to stand, snatching at the tea with a puckered mouth, as if it would bite. Nolan made smacking noises, loud and vexing, said:

'You're in the video game, Mr Brady.'

'Yeah.'

'Oh I do like a good film.' He pronounced it 'fill-um'.

'Me and the missus, we like nothing better than to put the feet up, have a curry, then a box of Dairy Milk for afters.

Though I suppose you'd have a sturdy young lad with yours.'

James threw me a look and Nolan bit down on a marietta, continued 'Oh sorry Sarge… didn't you know… ? Our Mr Brady is an arse bandit – a bum-boy… yeah, a pillow-biter in the flesh, so to speak. A bit of marg' would go a treat on these.'

He smiled and showed surprisingly fine, even, white teeth. Didn't add any warmth to the smile. Over the next few minutes he ate six biscuits, crunching down hard on each piece. I counted… what else had I to do? Then he patted his belly, said:

'Oops! I've been a bit of a greedy guts I have. Right – now Mr Brady, no doubt you've heard of the Police Benevolent Fund?'

'Oh yeah.'

'Watch yer tone, laddie!'.

'How about if I write you a cheque… Inspector?'

He stood up, brushing crumbs off his pants and tut-tutted. To hear a grown man make such a sound is awesome. And to think, he was calling *me* names!

'Oh let's not bother with formalities. Cash will be fine… coin of the realm, eh? First Friday of the month… like catholics.'

I had managed to keep shtoom, let him goad me, but I figured one shot was merited, said:

'Like bribes, more like.'

James gut-thumped me with his elbow and I went down on my knees. Vomit washed in my mouth. Nolan squatted down, eye balled me, said:

'You're an 'ard 'un Brady, eh… ? But this isn't the Scrubs. I'm the guv'nor here. If I whistle, you ask, What tune? Am I getting through to you, asshole?'

I nodded. There are times when it's best to be macho, to shovel the shit right back. This wasn't one of them.

I could smell the biscuits off his breath and see the particles stuck in the fine teeth. He stood, said:

'That's it then. Don't get up son, we'll see ourselves out. And tell that jungle-bunny mate of yours not to nick motors on my manor. Makes me look bad. Well, got to fly… toodle -pip.'

There's nowt as queer as folk.

My old man used to run that by us. Fucking wisdom of the ages, by gum. From a man who rated Yorkshire pud as a culinary achievement.

5

Reed had asked once, 'This depression man – how it be?'
'Be fucking rough is how.'
Mania is the ultimate rush. Energy and euphoria hit
fever pitch. A racing mind moves in a whirlwind pace and you
become the original motor-mouth – gunning out verbals at
hectic mode. Physically, little sleep is required and a supernat-
ural energy takes over. The next stage is delusion and you can
feel all powerful – all intelligent – all wonderful. Like a
Thatcher.

Depression is the exact opposite. Loss of energy, feelings of
worthlessness, mental slowness, a shut down. It's not a
common ailment. What joins the two is that mania is followed
by depression. The doctors like to talk about 'episodes.'
'Attacks' are no longer PC. So when you're in the middle of
one, you, 'Phew, it's only an episode, that's all right then.' Yeah!
A shrink told me that about one in two hundred people are
prone to manic depression. This was a comfort? Oh yeah,
episodes are not frequent. Lithium helps me best.

When I'd explained all this to Reed he was quiet, then
exclaimed, 'Jeez, what a bummer.'

Quite.

My weapon of choice is a baseball bat. I kept one under the
bed. For all things Hackman. Gene made a movie called *Bat 69*.

Course, I didn't give a toss for him then, else I might have inscribed 69 on the top. The sexual connotation would have been value sufficient. But more likely not. This was the real McCoy, a genuine Louisville slugger with wood as smooth as Tony Blair. If I could gauge the manic feelings building, I'd get Reed to hold the weapon, but you can't always. No, not always.

Much as I appreciated the craftsmanship, I'd once made a guy eat it – and not with his mouth.

After Nolan had visited, I went to see Reed, told him the deal. He took it well, said:

'Let's off the fucker.'

When I told him the amount due on first Friday, he added, 'Let's off the fucker Friday.'

He could have done with some lithium himself.

I looked at the photo of Roz again, held it up close. As if inspection could bring information. Nada, nowt, zero. The thing they used to say: 'Only the winner gets the dinner.' If looks were the means, this girl was starved. As the Americans say, Who you gonna call?

Who else?

'Reed.'

'Talk to me, baby.'

'We've got a job.'

'Lay it out bro'.'

I did. Omitted nothing, not even the baseball caps. Reed said – I thought he said – 'Blood-claat.'

'What?'

And he said it again, louder. Yeah, I'd heard him right.

'Reed, are you stoned?'

'Don't get righteous bro'.'

'What the fuck is blood-clot?'

'It's a state of mind bro'.'

'Like Texas?'

Those sighs from him again. Like his theme song. Put a soundtrack to a life, I'd get the Sex Pistols' 'Never Mind the Bollocks.' I danced to 'Anarchy in the UK.' But all is profane, they'd regrouped. Alas, my life didn't have the space for such re-runs. Reed's track would be Vangelis, punctuated by sighs. Deep... yeah. Reed had tried to explain BEV. Black English Vernacular or, quite simply, black-speak, he'd said:

'There be a whole new vocabulary of Niggaz – Buck – Whylin.'

I'd given an informed, 'What?'

It meant black men talking. Lest he now go totally black on me, I cut to the chase, asked:

'Are you free to begin tonight?'

'I be free.

'Okay, see you here 'round nine.'

Anything else?'

'One thin'.'

'Yeah.'

'When I be getting me baseball cap?'

For the next three nights we trawled through the Brixton clubs. The modern version of hell might be Railton Road on a wet Wednesday night. Milton would be glad of his blindness.

Thronged through the hustlers, pimps, transsexuals, transvestites, muggers, junkies, dealers. The signs that read – 'IF IT SWELLS? RIDE IT.' What Travis saw from a windscreen in *Taxi Driver*, we saw up close and reeking. *Mano el mano* with the waste that comes behind. Reed's colour may have got us in but my mania got us out.

He said, 'We be doin this wrong bro'.'

'Too easy-going... you want to crack skulls?'

'No... eee, we's got to put down some incentive.'

'Pay the bastards, that it?'

Laid the money and the promise of more all over Coldharbour Lane. We found her on Friday.

Ballistic is a word of mouth joint. Never advertises and never needs to. You have to be connected to get to the door, and connected plus loaded to get in. Reed had the appearance of both.

Half way down Electric Avenue, it kept a dilapidated front. Inside was plush – red and white leather, huge dance floor and circular stairs to the bar. We headed up.

The clientele was predominantly black and I looked...
well... white. Me 'n' Roz. She was behind the bar, dressed in
white leather micro and red see-through blouse. Truth to tell, in
the subdued light in that place, she looked pretty okay. A huge
guy in a tux caught Reed's arm, asked:

'Elias... that you?'

'Sure be.'

'Wha'ch you be thinking, yo' bring a white boy here?'

I pushed forward, 'Hey, nobody brings me anyplace.'

Reed shot me a look, moved the guy to the side... had some
words. Then back to me and before he could start, I said:

'Don't do me no favours.'

'Yo' all lighten up bro', yo' want the girl or a lynchin'?'

'You think I'm afraid of that fat fuck?'

'I'm afraid you not, now shut yo' trap... hear?'

He pushed me into a chair and moved to the bar. I watched
him talk animatedly to Roz. She looked over then nodded her
hair. Reed came back, said:

'She be here in a mo' – now yo' be cool... are yo' cool?'

'As ice.'

Something else was eating him.

I asked, 'What's eating you?'

'De girl – de white chick, she belong to Leon.'

'Who's Leon?'

'Uh... oh... here be Leon.'

A build-up like that you expect the point man for the grim
reaper.

What he was was small and almost insignificant. Dressed in
a blazer, white shirt, grey slacks, he wore pince-nez. His age
was indeterminate. You'd believe sixty, but fifty was an option
too. If I knew about ties, and I don't, I'd figure it to be one of
those regimental jobs.

Then you reached the eyes, cold as the Oval in December.
The glasses enhanced the metallic effect and, whoever was
home, was not to be fucked with. I decided to fuck with him
anyway. Reed jumped to his feet, said:

'Leon, this be mo' partner... Brady.' I stayed sitting.

Leon smiled, said, 'Don't get up Mr Brady.'

Yeah, he could do News At Ten, he had the accent. Put out his hand, I shook it. Like touching dead flesh and he knew I was thinking it, smiled more, said 'I am Leon.'

'You say that as if it's meant to mean something – don't mean shit to me.' As I said, no medication.

But he could roll:

'One likes to believe one has a small reputation.'

'I saw *Leon*...'

'Excuse me?'

'*Leon the Pig Farmer*.'

Didn't take too hot on that.

Reed raised his eyes to heaven.

Leon snapped off the pince-nez, rubbed the bridge of his nose, said in a tight voice, 'You're a foolish man Mr Brady... or crazy. But, as one has a certain fondness for...' He waved a hand vaguely to indicate Reed '...For Elias Rasheed, one is going to overlook your impertinence.' He waited for my response and I decided to forego it. The pince-nez was readjusted and he said:

'As I thought! Rosaleen will be with you presently. To demonstrate my largesse, drinks are on me. What is your pleasure?'

'Jack Daniels Old Number 7.'

'Capital! The black choice it is. Liquid smoke *n'est pas*.'

'Whatever.'

Then he walked away, to do power things, no doubt.

Reed slumped beside me, exhaled, 'Yo' a piece o' work, yo' know that?'

'But I have a nice telephone manner.'

'Sh... ee... hit! Yo' be messin wit' dee man.'

'No, no that's not correct. If I was messing, I'd have pissed on his shoes.'

Groan from Reed, then he sat up, leant close, said, 'Yo' mutha, yo' ain't on yo' medicine.'

Before we could get into that, Roz arrived carrying a tray with a bottle and those chunky glasses.

Reed said, 'Gimme dem drinks.'

I motioned for Roz to sit. She did, without any attempt to compensate for the micro skirt. It rode up to her crotch, showing heavy thighs.

I said: 'Show me your arms.'

'Are you a policemen? I'm not a junkie.'

I indicated her tattoo, said, 'Just being thorough.'

'Leon asked that I be courteous. How may I help?'

Cambridge had done its work on her accent but south-east London was going down shouting. The effect was what they call 'doing posh.' I was about to discover how her attitude was.

I said: 'Daddy asked me to find you.'

No expression, only, 'Now you have – congratulations!'

'Any message for him?'

'Yes, ask him to watch *I Never Sang for my Father.*'

'Lemme guess… Gene Hackman?'

Reed was doing damage to the drink. Another one who didn't know about sipping. One thing was clear, he didn't like Roz and he didn't seem to exist as far as she knew. Maybe that was it.

I asked Roz: 'Leon… he treat you okay?'

A smile of pure maliciousness. 'Oh yes, like a father.'

I had nothing more. The music seemed to have increased in volume, it was gangsta rap. Bounces off your skull like the worst kind of bad news.

She stood up and I asked:

'That noise, Christ, how do you stand that shite?'

Superior expression now, all of Cambridge crashing through.

'It's ethnic, it's… real.'

'Yeah,' I said, 'real fucking painful.'

And she was gone.

Reed said, 'Jeez Louise? Where yo' get DAT? Yo' white boys are weird.'

'It's ethnic, what can I tell you?'

As we took our leave, Leon materialised, put his hand on my arm, said:

'I don't expect to see you again, Mr Brady… understand?'

'What, is it a black thing… is that it?'

Outside, my head was humming. Volts of energy were cracking in my brain. I felt strong, randy and wired.

Reed said:

'Yo' all go home now … yo' hear.'

I looked at the crowds milling on Electric Avenue, heat emanating from the very ground, said:

'I am home.'

LEVELS

And final dream – on
sacred fear itself
I've feared
You are
but what we dreamt
from aspirations
basked in urgency
My mania
it is
my words out race
their meaning
every wasted time
and time
I never seem to get
to line the illness
clear.

6

In my early twenties, I challenged a shrink on the theory that mania and depressive 'episodes' are not frequent. In a voice laced with patience, he said:

'You don't fit the classic model.'

'Jeez, I'm sorry… If only I'd known!'

'You reveal, or rather exhibit, traits of the cyclothymic personality. That is a swinging mood from mild states of depression to mild states of elation. Alas, such traits can mean a person is more likely to be predisposed to manic depression.'

'So, it's like I'm serving an apprenticeship?'

He gave a tolerant smile, the type they develop from messing with lunatics. I never fit the bloody mould. Even my illness has to be of the renegade variety.

Before any diagnosis was ever applied, they categorised me as a delinquent. I did hard time in state schools all through my teens. The medics will tell you that stress leads to all kinds of mental breakdown.

The dormitories in those places, you'd hear the kids whimpering after lights out and the wetting of beds was commonplace. Come two in the mornings, you'd be dragged down to the bathrooms, the wet sheets wrapped round you, like early teenage shrouds. Bundled into cold showers, you then got to wash the piss from the sheets. I dunno if stress quite covers the feeling but it's in the ball-park. Yeah, it was definitely something you didn't get peace of mind about. Dysfunctional! How they managed before that showed up, I dunno. Can blame it all on dysfunctional. Jeez, what a word: the Prozac of the dictionary. Before it, we were plain fucked-up. Even the Americans were tired of the blame factor and have coined a counter measure – EXCUSE ABUSE.

My mother wasn't the full shilling and I guess being Irish didn't help. The predisposition to melancholia. She'd tell you in all seriousness that the rain in Ireland, 'Didn't mean it.'

Yeah.

She was the proverbial CIA – Catholic, Irish, Alcoholic – and vicious with it.

I read her spit in Daniel Woodrell. In the novel the son is asking his mother why she'd lied. The mother raised her chin to a belligerent angle, blew smoke at him and said: 'Why it should be obvious… I wanted to fuck with your head… pure and simple.'

The first time they strapped me down to administer shock treatment, I'd screamed before they forced the rubber dog between my teeth – 'Top Of The World Ma!' After I read the Woodrell, I figured you had an edge if you knew it. Not a big one but a start. My old man had a vaguely related idea. He said:

'Tells you in the good book son, you got to forgive them cos they don't know what they do. Well, the bastards I've met, they not only knew… they bloody planned it.'

7

The days after finding Roz, I went cottaging. If you don't know the term, you've not been reading your Joe Orton. It's cruising the public toilets – meet 'em and drop 'em. The original anonymous sex. Course it's risky, dangerous, dirty, and that's part of the thrill.

I took the show to north London, spread a little gravy over their potatoes. True, it has to be said, they do a better class of urinal – all Delft and institutional tile. You know you're in a shithouse. Condoms we have known. Leastways, I was hoping so.

Came out of the 'episode' to see what I'd scrawled on my bedroom in the yellow day-glo marker. I didn't need to read the writing on the wall, I knew I was hurting. Enough lucidity to call a mini-cab and get to the Maudsley. If they don't exactly know me, they are at least familiar with my history.

Two, three days… like that and they'd patched me back a bit and let me go. On the medication again, I began to stabilise. Time to call Jack. He was not a happy bunny.

'Where the bloody hell have you been?'

'Finding your daughter.'

'Oh.'

'Yeah.'

'Erm …you found her?'

'That's what you paid for.'

'Good man, I knew you were the right choice. Don't tell me over the phone… Copy down this address. I'll expect you at seven… alrighty?'

I copied down his directions – Dulwich, of course. The Kensington of south-east London, at least that's the way they tell it. I flicked on the radio, stabilising by the moment and caught the end of The Cranberries' 'No Need to Argue.' Hummed a bit with that. If I believed in omens, I'd have paid attention. It was followed hot by Bob Marley with 'No Woman No Cry.'

Enough!

I called Reed, told him to get his ass in gear, we'd to report to the boss.

He asked, 'Yo' all goin' to wear a suit?'

'Hadn't planned on it but hey, why not? I like a joke as much as the next guy and… I'm stable.'

'Sure bro'.'

'I'm serious Reed. I got a bit bent outa shape, but it's fixed – I'm on my medication.'

'Take mo'… a lot mo'.'

'I'm cool, I swear.'

'Yo' baby, yo' white… yo' ain't never gonna be cool.'

I hung up.

Being cool was over-rated, yeah… I could aim for style… now that's stable.

I have one suit. A timeless classic. Well, almost. Hand-tailored in Jermyn Street, it don't get finer than that. I got it in Oxfam on Kensington High Street, where the nobs and Arabs dump their shopping. The assistant said: 'Oh, how lucky… bespoke.'

'Be quiet!'

And shocked the bejaysus outa him. I had it fixed to fit in a booth on Clapham High Street, beside Wordsworth, the decent bookshop.

When I tried it on – hey, I was Tony Blair: same shit-eating smile. You get to wear a suit like that, you get a hint of why the rich are so smug.

One evening on Bedford Hill, a hooker said, 'Suit like that, you wanna play circus.'

'Play what?'

'I sit on yer face and you guess my weight.'

Like I said, a winner.

My father had five suits. It was the one extravagance in his northern frugality. I dunno if my mother's drinking was contagious but he began to drink too. The suits were identical and the object of my mother's wrath, her most vindictive scorn.

He always treated me fair. When I was nine, he lost his job as a hospital porter. My mother ordered him out. He was a better person drunk than most people are sober.

With the five suits, he went to live under Waterloo Bridge. In the tunnels there, he'd put on a fresh suit, then, when it was dirty, he threw it away. When he reached the last one, he stepped under the 9.05 from Southampton, the express.

I hated him cos my mother did. Then, when I understood who she was, I began to comprehend him. I read once that Hemingway's mother sent him the gun his father used to kill himself with. Cute. My mother would never have gone in for such studied viciousness. When she died, I had to clear out her things, dump all the empty bottles. I found a train timetable for arrivals at Waterloo. Maybe she thought he'd finally come up to speed.

I had a good look in the mirror, said, You're too handsome to let out, and began to read the satellite section in *Time Out*. They had a piece about sci-fi:

'Why anyone would actually want to watch men with no testicles in spandex outfits utter lines like, "The flux transponders nearly run out of euronium, captain" remains unexplained.'

I was with them – beat the shit outa me, too. Spandex!

If Nick Nolte can get his scrotum tightened in case he gets to do a naked love scene, then I'm way outa answers. The doorbell went.

An apparition in blinding white.

I said: 'Jeez!'

Reed in a cotton white suit, red shirt and red kickers. He said 'Sharp or what?'

'There's been a *Saturday Night Fever* revival?'

'Yo' be jealous bro', is all.'

'I don't think so.'

'Yo' see, dee man is impressed.'

'He'll certainly notice, I can guarantee that.'

Reed has a battered Cortina. What Leon would have called *de rigueur* for Brixton. It had a souped-up engine and we burned rubber to Dulwich.

Reed asked, 'De man, he know I be coming?'

'M… m… m?'

'He dunno?'

'Not exactly.'

'Well, be nice surprise for him.'

'Yeah, he'll be surprised, sure enough.'

He was – big time. The house was on its own grounds, well back from the road. Trees in an immaculately trim garden. TREES. The house said, You're talking big bucks here, none of your rent allowance shite in this neighbourhood. If you wanted to be obscene, try saying GIRO. Never heard of UB40, the group or the form. Did the house have a pool…? It sure had the attitude. Reed let out his breath, said, 'Home.'

Heavy iron gates blocked the entrance.

I said, 'They ain't going to open of themselves.'

'Yo' all try whistling? Why do I think yo' expects me to git out.'

'Helps the tone of the neighbourhood, Reed, if a *nigrah* opens them.'

'No shee-hit. See how it works – already yo' the white mastah.'

'Open the bloody things.'

We rang the doorbell and Jack actually stepped back on sight of Reed. Maybe he thought it was one of those home invasions.

Reed said, 'We be in the hood, mon.'

I added, 'Jack, this is my partner.'

'Oh... okay... erm... right... you better come in.'

The hallway was full of light. The last time I saw that much illumination was after ECT.

Jack paused, offered, 'You want to leave your jackets here?'

And the inference hung – Want to park the black too?

The combination of the lights and the whiteness of Reed's suit was dazzling. Into a sitting room choc-a-block with *Antique Roadshow* props. Plush armchairs that whispered, 'Flop in me.' We did.

Jack went to the bar and it was the full begonia, even had authentic wooden stools.

He said, 'Alas, I don't have your favourite tipple but, most everything else.'

Then he lapsed into a brogue, 'What will ye have, min?'

'A beer is good'

And Reed, awkward bastard, 'A Guinness.'

Jack made little trips back and forth, laying down coasters, bowls of peanuts, crisps, napkins. Reed raised an eyebrow, gave me the look. Finally, we were all squared away and Jack raised his glass, '*Slainte.*'

'Whatever.'

Silence then for a minute and Reed chewed peanuts, sipped the Guinness.

Jack broke, asked:

'Where is she?'

'In Brixton, she's working in a night club.'

'Is she coming home?'

'I don't think so.'

Reed suddenly interrupted. 'Hey mon, yo' be de twin fo' dat actor... dat Hackman dude.'

Jack suspected a rat, looked at me but Reed went on, 'Man, yo' do dat thin wit' yo' mouth... yeah... der, yo' dun do it again...'

And Jack beamed. Bought it full, said: 'Well, you're not the first actually...'

'I'm a believer bro'.'

I said, 'Yo'... Guys, can we get back to business?'

Jack composed himself, asked, 'Did she mention me?'

'Erm... yeah... sure.'

'Is she okay?'

'She's fine… truly… '

Jack took a large swallow of his drink, considered… then plunged:

'Can you bring her home?'

Before we could answer, he got up, walked over to a large painting. It had one of those little lights suspended above it. He shoved the frame aside and… yup, a wall safe. The middle-class aspiration realised. He did combination things, then pulled it open, took out fat envelopes.

Threw one on the glass table, 'That's a bonus for a good job… now this…' He held up a thick parcel, 'is heavy cash. It's yours if you bring her home.'

I hadn't touched the beer and my mouth was dry, probably the medication.

Reed said, 'There be a problem.'

'What kind of problem?'

I drank some beer… ah… cold and bitter, said:

'Leon… he's a black guy with juice who's protecting her.'

Jack lost it.

'You're afraid of some jumped-up nigger!' And realised… He looked at Reed, said, 'No offence. I mean, normally I'm not a racialist but…'

Reed indicated his drink, said, 'I's could go one mo' of dese black drinks, boss.'

Jack waved to the bar… 'Please, help yourself… okay…? So Brady, you're telling me you can't do it?'

'No, I'm not telling you that. I'm telling you it won't be easy.'

'What I just offered you… I'll double it. Now, is there still a problem?'

'No, sir.'

And then it struck me about the room. Mr Family Man, right? Not a single photograph, no family frame whatsoever. Nowt, nada.

You ever see those movies about the missing person, the hero always asks to see the girl's room, for clues.

I asked, 'Can I use the bathroom?'

Jack was seething, said, 'What! NOW you need to go, *now*?'

'If you don't mind.'

'Upstairs, second on the right.'

He didn't say stay out of the bedrooms but it was there. Oh yeah.

As I left, Reed was saying, 'I liked Gene in dem Batman movies.'

I checked the other rooms but they were locked. I was going to be clueless in Dulwich. In the bathroom I had a good wash, tried on some Joop aftershave. Nice. Then I opened the medicine cabinet. The usual crap at the front but I reached in behind and bingo... a thick bottle. Took it out and read the label – Temazepam. Uh-uh. The new name of oblivion for the housewives of London. No wonder his missus wasn't in attendance. I put the bottle back. All the towels bore Jack's initials and you have to be a special breed of asshole for that.

As I walked back into the room, Jack's voice was raised, 'I'm telling you it was the bloody *Superman* movies. Plus, it's not a period of his career I dwell on... okay?'

I gathered up the envelopes, stuffed them in my suit pockets, said, 'We'll be off then.'

'How soon can I expect a result?'

As Jack was closing the door, Reed leant back, asked, 'Yo' sure it was *Superman*?'

I drove, as Reed had laid into the Guinness. I counted six empties on the bar alone. Like I said before, I count. The shrinks say it's an outward sign of internal conflict. And I'd thought it solely an observation.

Reed said, 'We gonna need another dude.'

'Danny?'

'Mo' mon... Danny be good. What cho' wearing... yo' smell fine?'

I hit the radio for the country station. What a slice of luck, Iris DeMent but Reed moved the band, said, 'Sorry mon but I gots to hear de blues.'

'I thought you liked that rap shit?'

'No' me bro', I am de blues.'

Danny. The villain's villain. If there was a poll, he'd top it. Me, I didn't much like the bastard and he detested 'shirt-lifters.'

But… if you had to pick a guy, you'd be smart to go for Danny. Him and Reed went way back, so there was that. Danny was a burglar and a good one. He had only been caught once and that was down to a mate grassing him.

I fucking hate burglars. My own activities are far from legal but I hang on to the old dictum, An Englishman's home is his castle – or at least it's the building society's. I ever catch a guy doing my gaff over, I'll do him.

Danny was into a new caper. Literally an off-the-rails venture. Derailment. Once, twice a month a heavy goods train was knobbled. He got the call and as the looters went for the surface stuff, he'd select choice items with high street return. The month before, there'd been three derailments. One hit the front pages, because the cargo was wine. Bottles of plonk littered all over the tracks. There wasn't a home in south-east London without a nice Riesling to go with the fish fingers. As a burglar, Danny had access to the good things in life. You want passports, credit cards, driving licences, weapons… Give him a bell.

We'd need weapons. It wasn't as if Leon was going to hand over Roz if all I had was attitude. Yeah…

I said to Reed, 'No frills, no major strategy. We go in, we grab the girl, and we're outa there.'

'Leon's gonna know it be us.'

'Sure.'

'He gonna come after my black ass first.'

'I hope so.'

I had a plan for after. To fly to San Francisco and meet Armistead Maupin.

'Tales of The City' was my literary lithium. Calmed me down when the meter was pumping overload. Madrigal says in these: 'When I retire I'm going to buy a small Greek island.' Then she thinks a bit and adds: 'Well, maybe a small Greek.'

I had it all down in my head. I'd be sitting in Fisherman's Wharf, my face lightly sun burnt after the day trip to Alcatraz. A margarita in my hand and weejuns on my feet. Very soft battered ones. Armistead would stroll in and I'd take off my aviator sun-glasses, give a lazy smile and say, 'My Man!' Now… there's cool.

The phone crashed into my reverie.

I was not best pleased, snapped into the receiver, 'This better be good.'

'Tone... that you... it's Jack?'

Fuck.

'Wotcha want, Jack?'

'An explanation, very possibly an apology.'

'For what?'

'You bring a nigger into my home, you want to comment on that fella?'

'Yeah, I can comment, he's my friend, how would that be?'

'You couldn't find any white friends.'

'Nah, they were all like you.'

Silence, then...

'Look... Tone, I've got off on the wrong foot here. Let me make it up to you.'

'How would you do that, Jack?'

'You like Cliff Richard?'

'What?'

'I thought you might, well... when this is all over, I'm treating you to the best seats at the Hammersmith Odeon. A one-off reunion of Cliff and the Shadows, what do you say now, Mister... eh?'

'The Shadows!'

'We'll make a night of it, have a late supper at The Savoy.'

'Wow.'

'The sooner this is over, the sooner we start partying.' He said that in the American way.

'I'm humming "Summer Holiday" already.'

'You like that? Me, I love "Miss You Nights".'

'Well Jack, much as I'd love to stay swappin' classics from Cliff...'

'Of course... no hard feelings on the nigger then?'

'Jeez... bye Jack.'

8

Reed left a message.

'We be toolin' up, bro'. Danny's at Seven. Yo' all gonna need mo' than a bat and an attitude.'

I was going to wear the suit but you can have too much of a good thing. Plus, I didn't want to piss Danny off from the out. I resolved not to needle him.

Took my medication. My past was littered with the baggage of manic-depression. See the highlights…

hospitals
insanity
psychotic irritationality
the compulsive spending
and the part I dwell on least,
the suicide attempts
and yet…

When the elation hits, Jesus, it's like nothing on earth. Fireworks not only go off, you are the bloody fuse. A doctor reprimanded me on lust one time. It doesn't seem that it's a sensuality of white intensity razor cut to the soul of sex itself. Junkies say heroin is like kissing God. When elated, I am God and want to kiss the world.

You feel so fucking marvellous. You think you'll explode…

… and you do.

Cos there's no slowing down. That song...

'Fly me to the Moon'

Well, all the way over to Pink Floyd's dark side there.

Course, no one can keep apace. It's like a cobra on speed. Get outa the road, fast.

Then, the crash... oh shit, it's not the bottom of the pit. It's below that, scraping further down. A bleak nothing landscape of pure desolate emptiness. That's the destination, to dwell there in all yer days.

So I took the lithium and headed for Danny's.

He lives in Meadow Road, not far from the Oval. You can hear the crowd roars during the Test series. A one-up, one-down terrace house, as re-converted by yuppie values. Brass knocker in the shape of a mermaid.

I like that.

Gave it a fine wallop. A girl of sixteen... or maybe thirty-two... slim, dark hair, black Levi's and one of those... (halter-tops, are they?)... nice smile... opens the door.

'Mr Brady?' she asks.

Jeez, how old is that?

'How d'ya know I'm not a Mormon.'

'Bad teeth.'

'What? I frigging pride myself on those pearlies. Brush 'til I bleed with that tooth-whitener. The paint off a gate job. My face obviously showed all the shock.

She laughed, said, 'I'm winding ya' up, you have nice teeth, come on in, I'm Crystal.'

'Hello Crystal.'

I liked her. Mouth without malice, a rare humour. Danny was in the garden with Reed. Both in track suits... team players, eh? The fruits of derailment.

I said:

'Yer daughter let me in.

Danny's face tightened and Reed laughed.

'That be his old lady bro'.'

'Oh... and there was me thinking I'd interrupted her homework.'

Danny dropped in a deckchair, said, 'Least ways she's female, eh Brady?'

'Or will be when she grows up.'

Reed threw his hands in the air.

'Yo', guys – nuff of dis shee-hit.'

Danny shrugged, then:

'Crystal, bring a cold one for Tone…' He looked at me, asked, 'Yeah?'

'What the hell,' I said.

'Yeah.'

After I got that, I sat and Reed said, 'I dun told Danny what we be planning.'

I nodded, asked Danny, 'You in?'

'Sure, but we can expect deep shit from that guy, he's a serious operator.'

'You leave Leon to us.'

'Didn't mean him, it's the Paddy, he's no fool.'

'Naw, no worries.'

I was wrong of course.

Danny asked how I planned on it going down.

I launched forth:

'We'll need CS gas, a van and luck. All you need is to make sure the engines running and stop for nothing… Okay?'

'Sure.'

'That's about it. Once we got here, we deliver her to Dulwich, collect the cash and avoid Brixton for a bit.'

Reed said, 'I gots me a thought.'

'Shoot.'

'Let's keep the bitch.'

Danny laughed.

I didn't, asked, 'Keep her?'

'Sho', we tell de man she be kidnapped, he pay to git her back, she his daughter.'

'Jesus.'

'An… we's offer her back to Leon. Gits him to pay too.'

'That's crazy.'

Danny said, 'I like it, get 'em both to cough up.'

'Okay, Reed, say I'm daft enough to agree. Who gets her… Leon or Jack?'

'I dunno bro', I be making dis up as I go's along.'

Already I was thinking, it was just manic enough to work.

We had a warehouse for storing videos. Reed and I had sometimes crashed there and it had the essentials...

Electricity

Shower

Bed

Small cooker

Yeah, I could get to like this.

Reed smiled, said, 'Yo', like it... yeah, yo' like it a lot.'

I repeated, 'Make both the bastards pay.'

'It's evil bro', real fuckin' wicked.'

Danny thought so too, shouted, 'Crystal, bring a rake of cold
ones, honey.'

9

Danny had the burglar's pre-requisite: invisibility, or as near as matters. Unless he spoke, you didn't notice him. Every time I saw a police photo-fit, I thought, 'Danny.'

Yeah, he looked like everybody and nobody. He was about five-ten. I say 'about' cos there were times when he seemed to have shrunk. His hair was light brown, his features even and he weighed in about 160lbs. But I wouldn't swear to any of that.

The only distinctive feature was a cross he wore. He had all the necessary south-east London gear:

bent Rolex

Sovereign rings

gold ID bracelet

– the mandatory villain's outfit.

The cross was plastic and looked like it had been chewed. He wore it on a thin string of leather.

I'd said to Reed, 'What's with the Woolworth's plastic?'

'Man, dat be the third cross.'

This was supposed to enlighten me?

I asked 'This supposed to enlighten me?'

And got the story.

When Danny got grassed, he received two years and with the overcrowding, he was shuffled to the Isle of Wight.

Some guys, prison is a natural habitat, they adapt fast and even thrive. Others, it's the very last place they ought to be. Danny was the latter. Being banged-up completely freaked him.

Suicide was his desperate decision. One December morning, he'd wandered into the Chapel in search of heat… and down there, in winter, it is real fucking cold. Shivering, his eyes fell on a makeshift model of Calvary. The three crosses and little figures huddled at the base. The central cross had a figure and also the one to the right. The left was empty.

From Sunday School he knew one thief had taunted Christ. The other guy had been Mr Nice.

But could he find out the name of the rebel… could he fuck? He asked the chaplain who said, 'Concentrate on God and the Good Thief.'

Danny went back to the model and slapped the empty cross off it's base, thinking 'I'll get you outa this prison for starters.'

Shortly after, he got early release and believed the cross changed his luck.

I'd said, 'Not the full shilling, our Danny, is he?'

Reed was angry.

'Man needs something to believe in… to hold on to…'

'C'mon, a broken piece of plastic.'

'Yo' no be mockin' bro'.'

.357 Magnum or the Colt Python. Bloody cannons they are. Feel the weight of those suckers, you'd like two guys to hoist it. You stroll into yer nearest Nat West…

'This is a hold up. Hang on a mo' while I heft this bloody thing up to threaten you.'

Sure.

Guys like to throw the names of them about. When it comes to show time, you want some fire you can handle… unlike grief.

Crystal headed off to bingo shouting, 'Tar-a… see ya later.'

Like that.

Danny produced the hardware:

Browning automatics,

Glocks,
Revolvers,
.22s,
Sawn-offs
Reed asked, 'No Uzi?'

Danny grunted, not amused and Reed added, 'Dee homies likes de UZI.'

I said:

'They jam.'

Both of them were impressed. Danny said 'I didn't know you knew hardware.'

'I don't. I winged it, it's a macho line and see… you two went right along.'

'You're a real funny guy, Tone, hope you'll be more than winging it when you go up against Leon.'

'Yeah bro', dat Leon love to see yo' comin' wit a sense o' humour.'

I said:

'Fuck's sake, lighten up… all these weapons are making you ape shit.'

We divided up the preparations.

Danny to get the van, CS gas and balaclavas.

Reed to watch Leon's club, get a handle on the time they usually left.

Me to prepare the warehouse for our guest, get whatever might be needed.

We juggled round with this and Reed clapped Danny on the shoulder, said, 'Yo' Daddy be surprised to see his boy now, see what he be planning.'

Danny was feeling the drink, a pile of empty cans lay at his feet. I said nothing, kept my eyes on the weapons. A drunk is annoying, a drunk with guns is downright scary.

He had that tilt to his eyes, caught somewhere between maudlin and rage. I knew it, I'd been there if by a different route.

He said:

'Lemme tell you about my old man. Remember *Rawhide*? That fuckin' whip, jeez! He never missed it and every week as the credits rolled, they'd show that shot of the bloody ranch, he'd say, "Where do they get all them cows?" Every floggin' week, same daft question.'

He closed his eyes and you had to figure he was back at the ranch. We didn't know whether to laugh or just shut it.

So we shut it.

Then he jumped up, shouting, 'That's the gospel truth. Wait here, don't move, I'll show you exactly who he was…'

And off he went.

Reed said:

'Do you think he'll come back.'

'Oh yeah.'

He did.

Carrying a letter, a battered worn, faded page, pushed it at me, said, 'Go on then, see if I'm right.'

This is what it said:

Dear Daniel

By the time you red this, I'll be dead. The cancer has spread and I have terrible pains.

You have been a bitter dissapointment to me son. Where did I go wrong? The shame of you being in prison killed your mother. I enclose her wedding ring tho you'll probably sell it.

Before I go I want to help you. I advise you go to the Warden and tell him you've realised the error of your ways. Open your heart and he'll help you. It's not too late.

Your broken-hearted Dad.

What could I say? I said, 'Bummer.'

Gave it to Reed who read it, then asked, 'Wha' cho do with dee ring?'

'Sold it.'

'Ah!'

He opened a fresh brewski, had a mega swallow. One of those where you see the Adams Apple pump into overdrive. Quite 'orrible. The thirst he had, it wasn't for booze, but was I going to be the one to tell him? Was I fuck!

He said:

'Sundays! Everyone came round our house, uncles, aunts, neighbours and they'd all pitch in for the dinner. A chop, two veg, and roast spuds. Then they'd have a few drinks. Come evening, everyone would gather round the piano... wishing somebody could play it...'

I laughed out loud...

Then Reed said, 'Fuck it, it don't mean nothing... drive on.'

Danny smiled, said, 'You're my mates, my best best mates... let's get a curry, watch a vid'.'

Reed was excited:

'Yo' bro', let's git *The Domino Killings*.'

'What?'

'Gene Hackman, he wastes on all.'

I said nothing and Reed asked, 'Whatcha say my man, curry?'

'And... a box of Dairy Milk.'

If it was good enough for Inspector Nolan, then who was I to argue? As the scene with Mickey Rooney was rewound, Danny said, 'Yo' Tone, how would it be if I give you a present of the Glock? It's mostly plastic... lightest gun you can get.'

'Naw... I'll stick with what I know.'

Reed punched my shoulder.

'Git with de '90s bro, what's de deal with de bat?'

'It doesn't jam... know what I mean?'

They didn't.

If I were a man who appreciated irony, and most times I don't, I'd have to note that both Danny's cross and his weapon of choice were plastic. The moral being wasted on me. It's like Madonna wears forty-seven crosses and Mother Theresa wears one. A person could draw deep significance here. Me, I reckon, Go figure.

Time was when I was fascinated by coincidence and psych' books. A lethal combination. Ever come across Professor Karl Averbach? Not yer run of the mill TV pundit.

No.

He wrote an introduction to Freud's 'Future of an Illusion.'

'Coincidence begets mysticism, which begets religion, which begets sin and retribution, which begets repression...

guilt

psychosis.'

See, I could figure this shit out.

Shrinks have their war stories too. They're never happier than trotting out one of the standard yarns about manic depressives.

It gets them hot.

Usually they go like this:

A man believes he is the second most intelligent person in the world. He doesn't know the first.

Or the guy goes into a department store, charms the sales girl and buys every tie they have. Course he comes back later claiming he's been conned. He has, but not by the shop.

The best book has gotta be 'An Unquiet Mind' by Kay Jamison. Not only is she professor of psychiatry at the John Hopkins Medical Centre in Baltimore, she is also manic depressive. This lady writes from *inside* the barrel of the gun. In her own words, she was 'a raving psychotic.'

On one London spree she spent a small fortune on books because she liked the covers and magically, 'Twenty Penguin books because I thought it would be nice if the penguins could form a colony.'

I understand that completely.

Recovering alcoholics call it identification. Me, I figure she was reading my mail. 'Lithium,' she said, 'prevents my seductive but disastrous highs, diminished my depressions clears out the wool and webbing from my disordered thinking, slows me down, gentles me out.'

Oh shit, how I love the concept 'Gentles me out.'

Fuck knows, I been all kinds of heavy duty attitude all my born life but I've never been gentle.

And yes... I do miss what I never had.

Ever get your cod 'n' chips in newspaper? Cover them suckers in salt 'n' vinegar like there was no such thing as nutrition, put yer face down in 'em and breath that scent... like the scores of childhoods you wish you had, like a love you've never experienced.'

But hey, I'm getting manic here. End of the day, they're just chips and when you're done, you ball the pops and sling it in a wide hook shot. Sometimes it hits the bin.

A Jewish sailor… trolling on New York's Upper East Side
said it best:
'Oh Lord God of Abraham
Keep me Alive and smart –
the rest I'll figure out for myself.'

10

Next day, I treated myself – had me a rent boy. Done him to the music of M-People. So what if I'm fifty plus? I still listen to what's happening.

I didn't get him off the street. I went through the classifieds in *Gay Times*, got one who was available on a mobile, for fuck's sake and made house calls. He arrived at 4.30pm. All blond scraggy hair, torn jeans, ripped T-shirt and Armani leather jacket. Designer rough trade.

I offered him a drink, he said, 'Got any mineral water, sparkling… with a hint of lemon.'

'Sure.'

I poured it from the tap, added a shot of fairy liquid and figured he could imagine a lemon. Course he never touched it, they never do. Then he read the riot act.

'No anal. No bondage…'

And I interrupted, said, 'Hey, no talking.'

Had him quick, paid and we were all through by 4.55pm. I said, 'Don't call us, we'll get in touch.'

Can't help wondering if that's where the term 'bum's rush' derived from.

I don't regret too much. But I wished I'd told Jack the old story about *Bonanza*. How Lorne Green, as a fifty-year-old had four sons who were all forty-five, each born to him by a different wife and worse, who had all died giving birth.

…And no one noticed. A more innocent era or just plain stupid? Bit of both, I guess.

Time to prepare for Roz. I went into Boots, looking for a likely candidate. Got her, a middle-aged assistant… okay, *my* age. A Rasta was ahead of me, so I stood patiently. It had to be her. He had dread-locks all down his back and kept bursting into giggles, near convulsed with hilarity. Eventually, he shuffled away without a purchase. But she was good, didn't lose it.

I got right to her, said, 'I'll have whatever he's taking.'

And she hesitated, then smiled, said, 'I don't think that's on prescription.'

Okay, I began: 'I wonder if you could help me. My daughter, she's twenty and due to come outa hospital. She's coming to recuperate at my home and I'll obviously need all sorts of things for her… you know, like women's stuff.'

A moment…

'And her mother?'

Coup de Grace time.

I lowered my eyes, said, 'Her mum was taken from us… I…'

Then she took over:

'I understand. Shall I presume she needs a little of every-thing?'

I looked at her name tag, said:

'Thank you, Betty.'

It took some time so I tested the men's aftershaves. By the time she was ready, I was smelling good enough to eat. She handed me a huge carry bag, said, 'I think that'll do the job.'

'You're so kind Betty, you put the B back into Boots.'

'B?'

'Beautiful.'

Awful shit I know, especially as I had to run the same gambit in British Home Stores for the clothes. Then I hailed a cab, took it to Balham.

Our warehouse is situated near the rear of the Argosy store. They do mail-order and so do we. It's roomy with boxes piled high to the ceiling. An Arthur Daley wet dream. Best of all, you could scream your head off, no-one's going to hear.

I fixed up the camp-bed, laid out the parcels, then looked round. If I swept the floor, put up some chintz or, even better, gingham curtains, it would be downright cosy. Instead I thought, Fuck it, and got out of there.

Reed did his surveillance; Leon normally left round two in the morning. A minder walked with him and Roz to their car, which was parked a little down from the entrance.

Okay.

Danny got the CS canisters, the van and the balaclavas. The van was a transit, beat up and dirty.

I asked, 'Does the engine stall?'

'Nope, it's in good condition.'

Reed tried on the balaclava and said, 'Shee-hit, dis mutha be hot.'

Amazing, you put one of those on anyone, they immediately turn sinister.

He asked, 'How I look?'

'Evil.'

I wondered how Betty from Boots would fit one. Give a whole new agenda to the business.

11

We decided on a Thursday, not too busy, but not slow either. In there was a safe mix and we hoped this was it.

I gave Jack a bell.

'We're about ready to roll, you'll have her back by Friday.'

'Oh, thank God.'

'You want us to bring her straight to Dulwich.'

'That would be best, I sure appreciate this fellah. You'll find Jack Dunphy is a good man to be on the right side of.'

'So I hear.'

'She won't be hurt, will she, I couldn't bear that?'

'You have my word, Jack.'

'I'll remember you said that. Good luck then.'

Bit of bad luck the moment I put down the phone. The door bell rang and I figured Reed.

Figured wrong.

Nolan and his Sergeant. They barged straight in and Nolan said, 'Put the kettle on, there's a good boy.'

I didn't need the aggravation, so I went to the kitchen. I could hear the bastards poking round. The CS and gear were in Balham. I brought two mugs of scalding tea into the sitting room.

Nolan said, 'What, no bikkies?'

'All out, I'm afraid.'

He gave the big smile.

'Hey, don't be afraid, Tone, least not of that.'

I thought about San Francisco. Maybe before I left, I could pay Nolan a visit. The Sergeant didn't bother me, just one more asshole but Nolan got off on the game.

I said:

'You'll get yer money, what's the problem?'

'Problem, there's no problem... this is a social call. Cultivate good community relations.'

'Oh, is that what this is?'

Nolan stretched out on the sofa, his size nines up on the cushions, said, 'Not sure I care for that tone... eh, there's a good one. Tone's tone!'

The Sergeant gave a laugh. Like I said, asshole.

'You don't want to play cheeky buggers with me, son... oops... oh dear. What have I said? He'll have me up before the Gay Rights Board, eh... ?'

I said nothing.

Then he swung his legs off the sofa, stretched and stood up, said, 'I hear you're tight with Jack Dunphy. Now there's an interesting friendship. One thing puzzles me though, mebbe you can evalidate for me... ?'

'What?'

'Oh Jack, bit o' work he is, but he's noted for his homophobia. Lemme translate that: Nancy boys, pooftas, they get right on his tit.'

'So?'

'Good answer boyo, front it out. Thing is, how'd he be if he got a call, heard his new mate is light on his feet, eh?'

'Go ahead, see if I give a toss.'

Nolan prepared to leave, said:

'Word to the wise, me old china: you get some biscuits cos I'll be round and I do hate tea on it's tod.'

After they'd left, I took their mugs out to the yard. Beat the be-jaysus outa them with the bat. Childish... ? Sure, but it felt good. I debated telling Reed about their visit and decided not to. We'd enough players as it was. He'd worry and I needed him focussed.

Back inside, I turned on the radio, Golden Hits Show. Here were the Tremeloes with 'Silence is Golden.'

Now there was yer omen right there. So it was in falsetto and real hard on the ears but you took what you got…

My old Mum, she's talked some shite in her time but everybody has a moment, except for Mark Thatcher of course.

Before she died, I heard her lament into her bottle of milk stout, 'Once, just once, I'd like to have a blessing that's not in disguise.'

Cri de coeur.

I have no problem collating information. I can retain it but I have an uncanny knack for misusing it. 'The Bell Jar' by Sylvia Plath. Not exactly light reading but she lived on the same block of desolation as me. In the novel, she describes the concrete tunnels leading to the room where they strapped you down for ECT. Her descriptions were truly horrific. But, she warned, on the morning you were due, you didn't get breakfast.

So I was forewarned. The first time they put me away on a section, I knew what to watch for. A Tuesday morning, no breakfast today. For hours, I shat and shivered… waiting. Come lunchtime, no show. Steeling myself, I asked a nurse and she laughed out loud.

'Good Lord, no, dear. We just forgot to feed you.'

Course later, they came and often, breakfast or not. True too that I got to appreciate, if not relish, the voltage. After, you're nobody… you remember nothing; it's like being mentally stripped. There is a comfort to be had thus.

SHOW TIME!

12

We met at the warehouse. Reed looked round, said:
'Yo' went to trouble fo' dis cow.'
'A little.'
He produced a bag, said, 'I's went to trouble too… see…'
And he flourished two of those rubber face masks.
1. Maggie Thatcher,
2. John Major.
'Dos balaclavas… ain't no style...... dese be cool.'
I said, 'Don't tell me, I'm Major… right?'
Danny was well chuffed.
Reed added:
'See bro', I be comin at Leon, it be the black nightmare in de flesh, Maggie comin fo his black ass, like she said.'
'I never heard her say that.'
'Course, yo' be white, why fo' yo' gonna hear it?'
Made sense.
'Yo' gonna be Major, cos yo' comin up behind. Ain't no blood ever see dat cat coming.'
'What about Danny, doesn't he get to play?'
'Look at him, he bland and smug… a natural born Tory… dat dude be bred to rule.'
So the Tories went to Brixton, if not in triumph, at least in a van.

We were a little down from the club. Danny at the wheel, me in the death-seat and Reed sitting on the gear box. It was 1.30am. Lots of action on Electric Avenue, even for a Thursday. The radio was playing low, late-night golden oldies.

What is it, the radios getting off on constant reminders of my age? If you remember Woodstock, it's time for the knacker's yard.

Oh yeah.

Now they were playing Village People, four clowns in construction and Indian outfits. Hard hats and harder asses. Danny said:

'Your crowd, yeah!'

'Sure.'

Unconsciously, we joined in and not a bad little three-part-harmony, culminating correctly each time on:

Y

M

C

A

The Fun Boy Three, armed to the teeth. I was thinking, when I got home I'd watch *Death in Venice*. Salivate over the blonde guy.

You see some odd sights in Brixton. An old wino passed, with those sandwich-boards strapped on, front and back.

Front: *Vengeance is Mine*

Back: *Jimmy's Auto Repairs*

You don't see black winos.

Reed said, 'There go de neighbourhood.'

I made my point about winos.

Danny said, 'It's like you don't get yer black serial killers either, know why?'

We didn't.

'Cos they can't count!'

Silence…

Then: 'No offence, Reed… okay mate?'

'Dat what yo' mutha say when I give her one.'

Where this fandango might have gone, I dunno, because just then the club door opened and out came Leon, Roz and the minder.

I shouted:

'GO, GO, GO!'

We let them pass the van and Reed went out the back. Pulling on the mask, I opened my door.

Danny said:

'Make it Major.'

Reed walked right up to Leon, gave him a full CS blast then side-stepped and the same to Roz.

I swung the bat, connecting with the minder's right knee, heard bone go. Then I stepped round, put a dose of CS in his face. He was roaring like a stuck pig.

I clapped the back of my hand on Roz's neck and caught her as she fell. Losing the bat, I shouted:

'Get her bloody legs!'

And we slung her in the van. Leon was fumbling blindly as I went back to get the bat. I up-ended and shot it into his stomach.

That's all she wrote.

We were burning rubber and on to Camberwell New Road before I could exhale. Procol Harum were doing 'A Whiter Shade of Pale'.

Well, they would, wouldn't they?

You know how an expression enters the public domain. The *Sun* shows it on the front page, a Royal is caught flaunting it and bingo, it's everyday speech.

From *Minder* we got:

"Er indoors.'

Dick Emery gave us:

'Oo, you are awful.'

Larry Grayson:

'Shut that door.'

Liz the Biz:

'*Annus horribilis.*'

Yeah. Like that.

Now Oasis gave us a truly awful one:

'What's the story?'

And the yobos answer:

'Morning Glory.'

The Gallagher Brothers up on stage, giving it large, and

finally you thank Christ you're not young… and have to fake liking those fucks.

We decided to watch Roz in shifts. With three of us, we could break it up comfortably. Reed had the first and I was to relieve him. Masks to be worn. I stopped off at McDonalds, ordered breakfasts to go.

The windows of the warehouse were double sealed. No one was getting in or out. I banged on the door. Reed opened it and I said:

'Where's yer bloody mask?'

'I no be wearing dat shee-hit.'

'She'll recognise you.'

'She be up at de Cambridge… yeah… ? How long 'fore she figure who we be?'

I didn't wear mine either.

Roz was curled up on the bed, but facing forward now. Her eyes looked at me. They were hopping with anger. No signs of *her* being intimidated.

I said:

'Sorry for the inconvenience but it's only for a little while. Here's breakfast.' I put it down beside her, said, 'What's the story.'

And she slung the breakfast across the room.

It splattered against the cardboard boxes, bits of scrambled eggs beginning a yellow descent. I opened mine, popped a sausage in my mouth, then washed it down with scalding coffee.

Reed said:

'Dese eggs be good, bro'.'

I had some bacon, nice and crispy and between chews, said:

'Rosaleen, you probably think being a girl gives you some protection. Like a man won't beat on a woman…'

I slapped her hard on the face, open-palmed and as her head jerked back, I back slapped her again.

'You were wrong, lady. Now first thing you do is clean up that mess… then you shower and we start over. You refuse to shower and me and the black boy, we'll wash you… okay?'

I'll give her this, she didn't cry. Then she moved off the bed and headed for the boxes.

I said to Reed:

'You push off. I'll catch you later.'

'Yeah, git me some z-s. Yo' want I call Leon?'

Roz said, 'He'll have your balls on a plate.'

I looked at her.

'That what they teach you up at Cambridge?'

'You'll be sorry, Leon will tear you limb from limb.'

Reed said, 'I be sorry already.'

After she'd cleaned up the mess, Reed added:

'When dis be over, yo' come over mo' crib, do me some cleanin'… be good for de home-boys, see me got white help.'

And he left.

She took the shower and I left a tracksuit for her. I went to the other end of the warehouse to give an appearance of privacy. Turned on the radio and caught the news. No word on Brixton. Leon hadn't reported it. Quiet surprise.

She emerged naked, posed… hand on hip, said, 'What are you staring at?'

'Fat thighs, you did right skipping breakfast.'

That got her into the tracksuit but she tried for a point, 'You probably prefer boys.'

'*Moi?*'

I made some fresh coffee and she took it, asked 'Got any ciggies?'

'Funny you should ask.'

And took down a box marked 'sponges.' Opened it up, pulled out a carton of B&H.

She said, 'Are they low tar?'

'They're hot is what they are.'

I found some matches and she was in business. Drew the smoke deep and exhaled with a satisfied, 'Ah…'

'You're done this before, miss.'

'Fuck off.'

'Oh hey, save us the coupon, I'm collecting for an electric kettle.'

She carefully extracted it then tore it into little pieces.

I said, 'That comes outa your allowance.'

Thus we passed my shift in aggressive spirits. She'd sulk, then ask about how long we'd keep her and… like that, sometimes I answered, sometimes I sulked. Had to give her another few slaps but other than that, it was no worse than any other first date.

When Danny arrived, I said, 'No masks.'

'Just be myself, that it?'

He had a pile of glossy magazines.

Cosmopolitan

Vanity Fair peeking out.

I said:

'What, no flowers?'

'Does she want some?'

'Get in, for fuck's sake.'

Roz was doing exercises, stopped, said, 'Another wanker.'

And continued her sit-ups.

Danny looked at me.

I said, 'I think she likes you.'

He approached her, said, 'Miss… I brought you some mags, I didn't know your favourite, so I got a selection.'

She didn't stop but called out, 'Jes–us.

'He turned back to me: 'Any trouble?'

'Naw, she's a sweetheart, plus… a slap gets her attention.'

He was indignant.

'I don't hit women.'

'Naw, you hit on them.'

Then a superior grin, the male animal in preening glory.

'Women wouldn't be yer strong point, Tone… eh? Not yer field, so to speak.'

'Gee that hurts. But do keep using my name, mebbe later you can give her my phone number.'

'Shit… sorry… Tone… erm…'

Roz was up now, interested, said:

'He's gay… I knew it…'

Danny shrugged, 'Sorry.'

I got ready to go, added:

'Sorry? That helps. Maked it all better. Phew, I'm so happy.'

I looked at Roz, her face shining in triumph, said slowly to her, 'Yeah… I go for men, but not wimps like Leon.'

'Bye bye, Tone, keep it in yer pants, big boy.'

Outside, I considered and had to confess, she won that one. Maybe it was the Cambridge education, gave her the edge. I'd have to go back to beating her I supposed.

13

I got my head down and dreamt of Village People. Jeez, nightmares I have known.

One time I tried to kill myself, I needed a rope. Well, I'm English, what did you expect… imagination?

The big hit at the time was
'Reasons to be Cheerful, Part II.'

Ian Dury and the Blockheads. There's a name, eh? The arse end of punk. Hugh Cornwell and the Stranglers were on their uppers and Chrissie Hynde wrote for the *NME*.

Days of Puke.

I'm not saying these events are connected. It's how it was. I'd watched *Gone with the Wind*. Of course the inference gets drawn. Vivien Leigh was manic depressive. I never got why Judy Garland is the gay icon, with Vivien there undawned.

And coming off a ferocious bout of euphoria, I had been fucking exalted! And ended exhausted. I bought and sold my car twice in one week.

After the Burning of Atlanta, I stood up and, in the great English tradition, went to the garden shed. Took the rope and coiled it over the beam. Put the noose around my neck and kicked away the chair.

The physical pain was like nothing I ever experienced. I hadn't done the noose properly and I strangled for minutes, but my neck didn't break. Got free finally, heavily bruised and mangled. I checked into the Maudsley.

A guy I was bopping one time, was into auto-eroticism. Strangulation to the point of orgasm and seemingly, orgasm like nothing ever before. It would frigging need to be. Course it frequently goes wrong and:

You come

and

You go

permanently.

No thanks.

So in this Village People dream, there was a noose round my neck and pulling on it, was Jack. What the Americans call 'yanking my chain.'

Came awake, drenched in sweat.

Fuck.

Reached for a cigarette, but I'd quit... as Reed might say 'Shee-hit.'

If you could put a soundtrack to manic depression, I'd have Jimi Hendrix with

'All Along the Watchtower.'

See Richard E Grant in *Withnail & I* bombing up the M1, all systems fucked, Hendrix blaring and him roaring at people to throw themselves under.

That's close.

But if you want to get the full orchestration, the full phantom band going full-tilt-boogie, you could do worse than U2 with

'I Still Haven't Found What I'm Looking For.'

You have to get the version where the gospel singers are doing back-up. Yeah... and keep a rope ready... you're in business.

I showered, put on a pair of 501s, scuffed tan work boots, Ben Sherman short sleeve and Adidas windbreaker. The working gay, ready to prowl, if not to rock 'n' roll.

Did some spraying with Lynx deodorant. I like that Africa number. Picked up the phone and called Jack. Answered on first ring.

Probably sitting by it...

'Brady?'

'Yeah, hi Jack.' (No pun intended.)

'Is she there… there with you?'

'Jack, there's been a problem.'

'Don't tell me about problems, put her on the line, what do I pay you for?'

'Jack, she's not here.'

I was sweating… had I expected it to be easy?

Wiping my hand on my 501s, the receiver was wet with perspiration.

He said, 'Spit it out, fellah.'

'Leon has moved her… says you can have her for a price.'

'How did he find out? That nigger of yours tell him?'

'Jeez, course not. He obviously did some checking, knows you're worth a few sov's.'

Silence, but I could feel his fury, a palpable thing.

He said, 'Ever see *Mississippi Burning*?'

'Yeah… but…'

'Don't interrupt me son, don't ever do that. I tell you… Brixton will be fucking burning.'

'Don't go crazy, Jack… you'll never see her.'

'What do you mean?'

'He says unless you pay, he'll turn her out and…'

'Turn her out?'

'…Erm… as a hooker and… that you can collect what's left offa Bedford Hill.'

Longer silence and I managed to get my damn jacket off. Jeez, how'd it get so warm.

I had to ask, 'Jack… Jack… you still there?'

'How much does he want?'

'Forty big ones.'

'When?'

'Five days.'

Big exhale of breath or rage then, 'Okay.'

'You'll pay?'

'Yeah.'

'You're doing the right thing, Jack. I'll let you know the details in a few days… don't worry.'

'I'm not worried.'

'Good… that's good… and Jack… you won't do anything…
er, reckless… will you?'

'Do your job.'

And he slammed down the phone.

I said aloud, 'There, that wasn't too bad, was it? Piece of cake
really.'

I tore off the shirt. Christ, I'd have to go back in the shower.
Even Lynx hadn't the protection for this.

Hunger came calling and I checked my provisions. Had…

dead cabbage

Two sus' eggs

Wilted sausages

Kellogg's Frosties

My cup overfloweth.

Time for a greasy caff. Heading for the Oval end of the
Brixton Road. A girl smiled at me. Precious little use at the best
of times but she was insistent with it. I figured, a hooker or
lunatic, said testily, 'Was there something?'

'Mr Brady, it's me… Crystal… Danny's wife.'

'Oh shit, I mean… hello.'

She laughed.

Like I said, I liked this girl and on impulse I asked, 'Want to
join me for a spot o' nosh?'

'Could I?'

'Course you could.'

The café specialises in lethal carbohydrates. The do-you-in
grub.

Lovely.

Half of the clientele said:

'Hello, Tone.'

'Tone.'

''Yo, Tone.'

They knew me.

The other half were sorry they did and said nowt. We sat by
the window, she said, 'Me ankles are freezing.'

'You don't have socks.'

'I thought it would be warm.'

The owner came over, said, 'Usual, Tone?'

'Yeah. Crystal, wotcha want?'

'Oh just a tea.'

'Go on, have a feed.'

'Do you think I could?'

I said to the guy, 'Two of the usual, bread and butter, large teas.'

Then I said to Crystal, 'Hang on here a sec…'

And I took off… got to the corner and yeah, the little market was there… made my purchase and got back, as the food arrived.

Talking big fry-ups…

…Sausages, two eggs, tomatoes, fried bread, bacon, hint of mushroom.

'Jesus' she said.

'Tuck in, girl.'

We did.

She took a sip of tea, said, 'Hot as Protestants.'

'Aren't they supposed to be cold?'

'Not on a Saturday night, not on the Ormeau Road.'

I didn't quite follow the logic, but decided not to ask. I was afraid she'd explain. She buttered some bread, popped a wedge of sausage in there, ate heartily. Grease leaked down her chin but she didn't mind.

Me neither.

Between bites she said, 'It's like being a kid again.'

I enjoyed eating but mebbe more, I relished watching her eat. Without any self consciousness or dainty moves, she got to the grub in the shortest, least fussy way. She ate with and for pleasure. How often do you see that? I eat like a convict. With total alertness, aware of all around me.

When she was finished, she let a loud belch, then giggled, putting her hand to her mouth, went, 'Oops!'

'Same again.'

She laughed out loud. The best sound in the whole world. She sounded like Dyan Cannon:

earthy

alive

passionate.

I reached into my pocket, took out my purchase, handed it across, said, 'For you.'

Her face was alight with joy.

'But… how… ? why… ? Oh, when you just went out. Can I open it now?'

'I insist.'

Two pairs of socks tumbled out, pink and red. Mickey Mouse on one set, Minnie on the other.

She leant ever and kissed me, exclaimed, 'You lovely man, can I wear them now?'

'Absolutely.'

She did, then presented her leg for inspection. Minnie smiled at me.

I said, 'Class Act.'

Then her face clouded – she'd have been a lousy poker-player – asked, 'Can I talk to you about Danny?'

'Erm… okay.'

'We've been together a long time, people would probably say we're co-dependant.'

Jeez, I thought, Everyone's therapy-literate. If you couldn't label it, it didn't exist.

I said, 'When I was young, we called it a good marriage… nor did we know anorexia, that we called poverty.'

She laughed, if not convincingly, said:

'And I love him. I'd die if anything happened. I know he's on some job with you and with Reed. I have such a bad feeling.'

'No need, nothing to worry about.'

'Will you mind him?'

'Crystal, he's a big boy, he doesn't need minding.'

'For me… please… without him knowing?'

'Okay.'

'Promise me.'

'Okay… I promise… on Mickey and Minnie's head… how would that be?'

'Thank you. I feel relieved now.'

Get me, eh? Giving my word out like a drunken sailor, with about as much control of consequence.

We stood outside the caff and she touched my cheek with her finger, like Barbara Streisand in *The Way We Were*.

She said:

'I don't know why Danny doesn't like you.'

'Yes you do.'

'He's so intolerant, he used to love Steve McQueen.'

'I'm sorry, did I miss something?'

'You know the rumours about him… with the motorbikes 'n' all.'

I laughed, said:

'Jeez, the bikes! Give you away every time.'

She didn't get it, so went back to the beginning. I wish I could.

She said, 'I like you.'

And off she went. I watched her down the Brixton Road. The flash of pink as she moved and said, 'Great walking.'

Bemused, I stepped into the road and *WALLOP!* a courier cyclist piled into me. It felt like a bad voltage of ECT.

All the crap they mouth about suddenly being struck by love, they might have a point. As I sat upright, the cyclist bent down, all concern.

'You okay, buddy?'

Saw these light lycra shorts and a scrotum that Nick Nolte would kill for… Met a pair of brown gentle eyes that mule-kicked my heart. He helped me up and I gauged him… about twenty-five… with Hugh Grant hair and the lean, sinewy body of a natural athlete. This guy would exercise cos he liked it. I said:

'I think I love you.'

'What?'

'Nothing… I'm okay… you okay?'

'Yeah… but the bike…'

We looked at it, the front wheel, buckled.

I said, 'Fucked is what it is.'

And he laughed. Jeez, what a morning! Apart from Jack, I was Mr Congeniality to the world. That and heavily bruised. My 501s were ripped and I could feel the beginning of a massive pain down my left side. He touched my shoulder and I know that touches can be deceptive. They can mean all or nothing.

He said, 'Can I do anything for you…?' The eyes locked on mine.

'Yeah, give me your telephone number.'

As he wrote it down, I added, 'Jill Clayburgh said in *Silver Streak*, I give good phone.'

He handed me the slip of paper, our fingers touched. Sing the body electric... *Oh Dios Mio*. Beyond chemistry, a red hot blend of splendour. I looked at the name...

Jeff.

Said, 'Well, Jeff, glad you ran into me.'

He lugged the bike on to his shoulder, said, 'I hope you'll be all right.'

'Jeff, I am fuckin A.'

As I limped off, I sure felt it.

Sometimes the movies seem more real than reality. Would it were so. They definitely have the better lines and can soft focus the best moments. Most things, I relate to them; whatever happens, I can pick a parallel scene to emphasise if not down-right embellish the reality.

Could I but write the script and slot in a happy ending.

Yeah, I'd like that.

I watch a huge range, from *Sebastien* to *Devil in a Blue Dress*. I draw the line at Peter Greenaway, I'm a buff, not a masochist.

14

Reed said, 'Maan, I got de blues.'
Well, I was edging the jackpot, nobody was going to rain on my parade.

I said breezily, 'What's going down?'

'I dun spoke to Leon, he shoutin' bout dee vengeance of de Lord.'

'Ah, he's pissing in the wind. Just remember, it's got *Jimmy's Autos* on the reverse. How much did you ask for?'

'Fifty large.'

'Sweet.'

'How we gonna collect, tell me dat, bro'?'

'We'll have him deliver.'

'I gots me a bad feelin', bro'.'

'You leave it to me, it's going as we planned.'

'Yeah… din' tell me bro', yo' plan fo' Dan-yell to be makin' moon eyes.'

'What?'

'Yeah, he be takin' wit de bitch … he think she be foxy.'

'I don't believe this shit, is he riding her?'

'Other way's round, bro'.'

'He's giving it to her Greek?'

'Naw, why fo' yo' no listen up, she be doin' him.'

'Are you sure?'

'Yo' all think they let me watch? I can smell it an' he looks like de cat got dee cream.'

'The dumb fuck.'

'What yo' gonna do now?'

'Think, I'm going to think... Okay?'

But I didn't. Leastways, not about that, not then. I was thinking about the Jeff-ster... about two tickets to Frisco... about... Screw Maupin... who needed him, anyhow?

I called Danny on the mobile.

Yeah, there was a spring in his voice, said, 'That you, Tone?'

'Yeah, how's everything there, any problems?'

'Naw, sweet as a nut, she's a good kid, I'm finding I've a flair for this.'

'What... babysittin'?'

'Good one, Tone.'

This is where I should have given him a bollocking, told him to get his act in gear. Like that.

What I did was:

'Danny, could I ask you a big favour?'

'Sure.'

'Would you do a double shift? Cover for me... ? I...'

'Hey, no need to explain, Tone. Glad to.'

'I really appreciate it, Danny. I owe you, okay?'

'My pleasure. You'd think this kid would be toffee-nosed what with Cambridge 'n' all but she's down to earth, a real ordinary person.'

I wanted to say 'Like Crystal', but I needed the favour more, said, 'Thanks again, Danny.'

'What are friends for... eh?'

And he rung off.

Then I called Jeff, arranged to meet him at eight. Jeez, I even loved his voice.

Splendid evening, the Gods smiled huge. Jeff had dressed for the occasion, white button-down shirt, dark chinos, imitation Gucci slip ons. Those I know cos we do a brisk business with Taiwan via Deptford. I didn't look too bad, either. Farrah slacks (c'mon, I'm over fifty) light polo neck, sports jacket. It was leather patches on the sleeve, to give the studied – if not studious – look. Yeah, I was a comer.

We had a drink at the Cricketers first. Probationary conversation, checking each other out. Couple of drinks and then off to an Italian joint at the Elephant. They do a mozzarella to die for. Ordered some Asti Spimanti and got behind that. I knew what he did for a living, he asked:

'What do you do? Good Lord, I don't even know what to call you.'

'Tony's good. Not that I am... least not if I can help it.'

The depth of my humour.

I was in the mild horror-zone of wanting to impress. A completely new take for me. My brain was delivering some impressive conversation but bright nuggets of repartee were mutilated into banality. Worse. I knew but couldn't stop.

'I'm in the people business.'

'PR, you mean?'

'Sort of, I get people what they need. Now can I get you another drink?' Scintillating.

He asked:

'Have you always been out.'

'More or less, it wasn't so acceptable in my day.'

'C'mon Tony, you're not that old.'

Loved him all right.

'What about you, Jeff?'

'Oh, I went to a very minor public school, buggery was compulsory.' I laughed out loud. Too loud. I didn't even find it funny, said, 'All that education to become a messenger.'

'Did you ever hear of Saki?'

'The Japanese drink?'

He laughed politely. Hell, we were having a high old time.

'Saki was a short story writer. An early Roald Dahl... he said, If you truly want a boy to become vicious, you have to send him to a good school.'

'And did you... become vicious?'

'I became an actor, is that the same?'

'I think so.'

We had a clever chuckle, just two guys chuckling away. He told me of bit parts in *The Bill*, *Eastenders*, and pièce de résistance, the lead in a building society ad. He asked if I'd seen it, I gushed, 'Jeez, is that you? I love that ad.'

'Well, it got me noticed.'

I'd never laid an eye on it but to be fair, it was probably terrific.'

'So now you are – what's the term? – *resting* on a bike... or you were?'

'Keeps the pecs in shape, I have to be ready for the call. I'm saving for America... if I could get to Los Angeles, I know I'd be big.'

I was fairly big myself. Had to hold back from saying about us going to San Francisco. Didn't want to scare him off.

When we came out of the restaurant, I asked, 'You wanna swing by my place? I'll show you my video collection.'

He looked like he might but then:

'Not tonight Tony, I've an early start, have to go and see if my bike's ready, it's in emergency repair.'

'Plus, you don't kiss on a first date, am I right?'

'It's not like that.'

'Sorry, just kidding... I'm nervous here... Okay, cut me a little slack.' He leant over, kissed me full on the mouth. Risky business at the Elephant Roundabout. The gay basheen prowl that area like the worst dose of disease. It got me hot again, the danger feeding the libido. Jeff hailed a taxi and as he got in, said, 'See, you were wrong.'

'*Moi*... wrong! You jest... surely?'

'I do kiss on a first date, call me.'

And he was gone.

I muttered, 'Call you...? I call you divine.'

15

Next day, I relieved Danny. He was full of bonhomie, if that's the word. Full of crap.

Talk about a warm welcome:

'Tone, good to see you, son.'

Like that.

Roz was sulking and jeez, I do love it when they do. She was wearing a fresh tracksuit and appeared... ready. Yeah, that's how she looked.

She said, 'Here's the local queer.'

I said, 'You're educated... right? Well, if you knew yer Derek Jarman, you'd realise that the word is not as offensive as you hope.'

Her lip curled, said, 'You're offensive.'

Danny was reluctant to leave.

I said, 'Don't worry. I'm not going to hit her.'

He said, 'Okay, then... bye, Rosaleen.'

Rosaleen!

He'd been gone maybe five minutes when I hit her. I said:

'Surprised? After what I told yer paramour? The thing is, I lied. You ever call me names again, I'll remove yer top teeth. Am I getting through to you, Rosaleen?'

I was.

Towards the end of my shift, I said, 'See how time flies when you're having fun?'

She'd spent her time reading and listening to a Walkman Danny had provided. Oh, and smoking, serial fashion. I could hardly see her through the smoke. Each time she hit a fresh pack, she'd carefully extract the coupon and meticulously shred it. Little piles of free offers surrounded her camp bed like sad heaps of confetti.

I suddenly jumped to my feet, slapped my forehead and went, 'Oh no!'

I like a touch of theatricality as much as the next thespian.

She flinched back, so I added:

'There was us, having a quiet day at home, having quality time together, and I clean forgot I got you a pressie.'

She said, 'I don't want a present.'

'Course you do.'

And lobbed a parcel. It landed beside her and she moved away.

I said, 'Go on open it… won't bite.'

Curiosity impelled her to cautiously approach the parcel and touch it, one eye on me all the while. A T-shirt tumbled out and she said, 'What... ?'

'It's a large, I couldn't help noticing you're packing some cellulite, but if it doesn't bother Lady Di…'

She held it up. On the front was 667

Triumphantly she turned, spat ,'You fuckin' moron, it's 666!'

I smiled, said, 'That there, that's the neighbour of the beast.'

Reed came storming in, agitation writ large.

'Bro', we's got to talk.'

'Sure… excuse us a mo', you play with yer T-shirt.'

I moved up to the door, asked, 'What's shakin'?'

'Me bro', de bloods dun come to my crib… wit' machetes, dun slashed it to shee-hit an' gone.'

'Leon's goons?'

'What cho think, they be lookin fo' mo' TV license? They be Leon's.'

'Jeez, lucky you weren't there.'

'Yah. I be born lucky.'

'Time to get serious, he's going to cough up now.' I moved over beside Ros, said:

'Let someone you love know you care.'

Me and Bob Hoskins both.

Asked Reed for Leon's number and punched it in on the mobile. Answered, said, 'Leon?'

'It is I.'

'Get this, you fuck.'

And tore a lump from Roz's hair. She screamed like a banshee.

I asked, 'Hear that?'

'I hear it, please… no further demonstration is necessary.'

'Hey, fuck-hole? don't tell me what's necessary. I'm holding a clump of her hair in my hand. You ready to rock 'n' roll, else I send you her wrist… the tattooed one… in a bag.'

'I'll do what you ask.'

'That minder you've got… have him at The Oval Tube Station at eight in the morning… with the money. He's to hand it to a *Big Issue* seller. Got that?'

'Yes.'

'That's fifty-two large.'

'I beg your pardon, fifty two?'

'Yeah, the extra is for re-decoration, know what I mean?'

'I follow you.'

'Yo'… bollocks, that's exactly what you don't do. Otherwise, I'll put the white meat to Roz here … how would that be… go where the black has been and boldly.'

'Afterwards, where is it you believe you can hide from me?'

'Gee, that's scary. Gotta go now, give yer bitch her bath.'

Reed was sweating, said:

'Yo' be losing it, mon.'

Roz was whimpering, said:

'You didn't have to do that.'

I shouted, 'People!… You… enough with the negative waves. If I have seen further than most, it's because I have stood on the shoulders of giants.'

I took Reed by the arm, said:

'Step outside with me a moment.'

'Yo' all gonna kick me black ass?'

'What? I'm not a violent man… I'm just another Ghandi with edge.'

Outside, I gulped in the Balham air, said:

'I have good news.'

'Yo' gonna shoot yo-self?'

'I've found somebody.'

'What cha be sayin'?'

'I think I might be in love.'

He stepped back, his eyes wide as a Stockwell barrow boy, exclaimed:

'Yo' be courtin'… you be dancin' and moonin' while dee hood be chasin' us with machetes?'

'You'll like him, he's different.'

Reed moved to go back inside, said, 'Dat medicine yo' be takin', it not be enough… we be fucked… dat what we be, how yo' plan to collect de money?'

'By courier.'

'De Lord have mercy – we goin' down.'

GOING
TOXIC

16

I went straight home, got a large hold-all and piled in the essentials:
1. Lithium
2. Baseball bat
3. Cash, a lotta that.
Also clothes, toiletries and Walkman.

Ready to boogie, called a cab and, moving fast, checked into a hotel off Clapham Common. Not a bad little place. Cypriot-owned, my room was large, bright with a shower. I could see the Common from my window. Spring or Autumn, I find it's vastness beautiful. If I opened my window, I could hear the ducks and it sounded like normality. I guess this would explain me best, that I'd gauge normality by the quacking of a duck.

Perhaps the best metaphor of all for a mind, wounded at it's centre.

Along the wall were the two basics for urban survival, coffee-making facilities and a phone.

Made an elephant black caffeine and chugged it, fast… too bitter, too raw… just how I loved it. Made another, getting mobile.

Originally, I'd had an elaborate plan to collect the ransoms involving Danny, Reed, Drop-bird; now I thought,

Fuck it!

And I'd go for the simple hit. It would work or not, but it would certainly be rapid.

Called Jeff, said, 'How you doin'?'

'Good… I enjoyed our evening so much.'

'I may be able to help you get to America sooner than you think.'

'Pray tell.'

I laid out the scenario and waited for his response. Damp… way down the enthusiasm scale.

I asked, 'Jeff, you're an actor, right?'

'Erm… yes…'

'Then act grateful. I'm helping you out here.'

'Sorry Tony, it sounds iffy.'

'Iffy… what's that, an Equity word, is it?'

'Don't be horrible.'

'Just be on time, son.'

And rung off.

I was crazy for him but that didn't mean I wouldn't put the wrath of *be-jaysus* his way. Keeps them focussed.

As I headed out, the guy at reception asked, 'For how long you be staying… Mr…?'

'Hackman.'

'Like the film person?'

'*Acrivos.*' (exactly).

He was delighted, near orgasmic. One Greek word and you're family. I learnt it at the Oval Kebab joint. I had some more but I figured I'd ration them.

He said, 'You speak Greek. I am Spiro, welcome to my home. This evening you will take a little ouzo with me.'

Shows my simmering paranoia but I thought he said 'Uzi.'

And took a moment to re-focus. Could have said, Oops, beware of a Greek bearing gifts.

What I actually said was, 'Thank you.'

And I was outa there. Needed to find Ben, the *Big Issue* vendor and while he was still sober. That wouldn't be much longer, if I knew Ben. I was, as the Americans say 'pushing the envelope.'

When times got very tight, Ben would drink surgical spirit. He called it 'An urge for the surge.'

Who was I to argue the toss?

On remand one time, in the psycho-wing of Brixton Avenue, they'd pumped me full of L. For days I did 'the largaktyl shuffle.'

That's like Frankenstein with DTs.

I found Ben sitting outside Kennington Park. On the bench reserved for winos. He had on the *Big Issue* uniform – warm coat, mittens, layers of sweaters, three scarfs and a blasted face. His hair was matted and thick. Like African corn-rows, save it was a result of sleeping rough. He was attempting a roll-up.

I said shrewdly, ' Ben...'

'Aw, *jaysus*... Brady... here, will you roll this whoring thing? I'm shakier than a Tory promise.

His brogue was thick as Sally Army soup. But the eyes were alert, blue and bright with a sadness of infinity. I did the cigarette, rather a neat job. Time in prison is not entirely misspent. Ben, like most Irish I knew, had an encyclopedic knowledge of startling information. Most of it useless and thus prized the more. I handed him the rollie.

He said, 'The blessings of God and His Holy Mother on you and yours.'

Roughly translated this means, 'Gis a tenner.'

I'd come prepared and produced a flat half-bottle of Paddy. I wanted him oiled but aware, said, 'Some *uisce bheata*?'

'Jaysus, you re a miracle on feet and you have the gaelic too.'

'My mother was Irish.'

'I knew her well.'

Ben was twenty-five. The chances of him knowing her were slim to none. But, I know how to play and answered, 'She always spoke highly of you.'

'And me of her – Leitrim woman was she?'

'Galway.'

'Ah ... Nora Barnacle country.'

'Who?'

'James Joyce's missus.'

He probably knew her too. Every one in Galway did. The Paddy was reverentially uncorked and he drank deep and open… waited… then a thunderous shudder racked him and he croaked, 'That's better now.

I watched as his eyes bulged and sweat torrented down his face. Then the eyes peaked and fell back to melancholy. He took a chaser and drew mercilessly on the cig'. We waited as the various poisons queued in his system.

Then he said, 'You know Brady, there's a theory that most of the world goes around asleep. Completely unaware of what's happening. Imagine that!'

I pondered then said, 'I've just come from Stockwell and can endorse it.'

He laughed.

'Jaysus, it's so dangerous there, the muggers travel in pairs.'

'I know them both.'

The bottle was finished and he said, 'Anyway, there's maybe five hundred people in the whole world who are awake and know what?'

'Erm… they don't pay their TV licence?'

'They're gay!'

I had no reply to this. So I figured I'd best get down to business.

I asked:

'How'd you like one hundred pounds? Buy the homeless a bit of time, if nowt else.'

'Who'd I have to kill?'

I laid out the details.

He listened then gave me a look of total concentration, asked, 'Is this dodgy?'

'Course it is, that's why you'll be getting a wedge.'

'Two hundred, so.'

'Hey, Ben… I thought we were friends.'

'Sure what's that got to do with the price of onions?'

'Okay.'

'I won't get hurt, will I? I wouldn't want to be beaten.'

'I give you my word, Ben.'

I was set to go when he said, more to himself:

'Joyce was always poring through dictionaries and Nora B asked him, "Aren't there enough words in the English language for you?" She'd a mouth on her, comes with being from Galway and he said, "Course there are, they just aren't the right ones".'

'You've read Joyce, have you?'

'Don't be coddin' me.'

17

I thought I'd swing by my home, see if anyone was keeping tabs. On foot, I cautiously approached the top of the road. An Audi swung in beside me, the window rolled down and Jack said, 'Get in.'

He was in the driver's seat and I slid in beside him. I said, '*Vorst sprung dorch technic.*'

It wasn't even noon and already I was into my third language. Then I noticed two huge men in the back. As fine a pair of thugs as you're ever likely to see. The type who run Bouncer Academe. Identical in their suits, silence and animosity.

I said, 'Lads.'

They said nothing.

Jack kept the engine running, it made a hum of real comfort. He was wearing a mohair top coat. An ugly garment and he had leather driving gloves. You have to be some pretentious fuck to carry that off.

He said:

'I hear you're a poof.'

Follow that.

I asked, 'Seen any Hackman films recently?'

Surprised him.

'No... I watched *The French Connection* last Wednesday, or was it Tuesday? Why?'

'*The Birdcage*, with Robin Williams… ol' Gene gets to drag-up.'

Jack coughed and then I felt an almighty wallop on the back of my skull. It bounced my face off the dashboard and it hurt, it hurt like hell. As my vision cleared some, I turned round to eyeball Thug Number one. His expression hadn't changed.

Jack asked, 'When is it I get my daughter?'

'Two days, it's in hand.'

He tapped his teeth with a gloved finger, said, 'I was reading up on kidnapping. The FBI's behavioural unit have been studying the relations of victims.'

'*Quantico.*'

I got another ferocious bang to the side of my head.

Jack said, 'I told you once, don't interrupt me. They found that once a person agrees to pay a ransom, that person has learnt something he didn't know. That he has a price, that he can be bought. Once he realises that, he becomes a very dangerous individual. I'd like you to consider this theory. You can now speak.'

'Why are you playing hardball. Aren't we on the same team?'

'Well, let's see… Firstly because you re a queer and I don't like queers. They're an abomination. Secondly, I want you to know where you rate on the food chain. Do you know?'

'I do now.

'Good, that's very good. Give him the brief case.'

Thug Number Two shoved a slim attache case over the seat. I took it and Jack said:

'Word to the wise, old son. If you're contemplating any independent action, I'll cut yer balls off and put them in yer mouth.'

I had a macho response to that but I kept it to myself. Two digs in the head are more than adequate. As they drove off I felt a flood of sweat cascade down my back. I wondered if Joyce had found words for that. I settled for, 'Shite crossways.'

Back to the hotel, avoided Spiro and into my room. Threw the case on the bed and shouted, 'I can see fucking India.' Opened it slow, row on neat row of new crisp bills. Was there forty large?

I'd say so. Did I count it?
No. Did I ring Danny and Reed?
No. Did it make me happy
It helped.

18

You'd think that knowing lithium solved my manic depression, I'd just take it and be grateful. But it's a constant struggle to do so. Part of me rebels against the daily task, against the idea of being medicated. There are some drawbacks too. It can play havoc with my concentration. Until the level settles, I can't read for any length. Shakes, it brings ferocious tremors and out of the blue. You learn never to use saucers or spoons and especially not to allow anyone to hand them to you. Else you see the horror on their face as the spoon does an Irish jig. Vomiting and nausea are part of the deal. You never get used to that shit.

How many times I'd been told that changes in diet, exercise, temperature and the level went toxic? The appearance is similar to drunkenness:

slurred speech,
no co-ordination,
throwing-up

and it requires immediate medical treatment.

Most of all, I missed the high. There was an ad for the dope movie *Rush* a time back. It went, 'Between the high and the buy'. No matter that the mania was frightening and lethal, I longed for its seductive beginnings. When my whole being glowed and I was smarter, sexier and supremely uplifted.

For a time I knew everything and felt everything, wanted to nail and be nailed by the world. Despite how that sonic track led only to hell and beyond, I yearned for it.

Being relatively okay and like most people is so fucking boring. There's the trap in all its alluring madness.

I'd set the clock for six and rose with it. Showered and coffeed and ran the plan again in my head. Full of loopholes and improbables, it leaked danger. That's why I felt it was a go. A basic simplicity can't be beat. Leastways, I was gonna find out.

My head hurt where the thug had hammered me. The length of my body was sore from the collision with the bike. Truth to ask, was I the right material for a derring-do caper? Part of me burned with vengeance. I wanted now to stalk Jack and do horrendous things to the thug.

A few years back the black mayor of Chicago was a strutting high flyer. His enemies bided their time and bile. Sure enough, he got caught doing coke and hookers. Disgraced, he went to prison for three years. On release, he clawed his way back up to re-election. When asked if he'd a message for his enemies, he said, 'GET OVER IT'.

I recited this now as a mantra. As I headed out, a sleepy eyed Spiro lifted his head at reception, said:

'Mr Hackman, you go early.' A trained observer obviously.

'Yeah, it's busy, busy, busy.'

'I give you breakfast?'

'No, catch you later.'

'You take caution Mr H.'

'Oh I surely will… *epharisto poli*.' Made his day.

At 7.55am, Leon's Minder arrived at The Oval tube station. He was carrying a black Reebok sports bag. Not best pleased, he glared around. People were milling about, traffic was bumper-to-bumper, the area was hopping. At eight, Ben came out of the café beside the newspaper stand. A bunch of *Big Issues* before him, like a shield. Walked straight up to the Minder, said:

'You've something for me?'

The Minder pushed the bag at him and Ben said, 'Sell a few o' these mate while you're standing there.'

Then Ben turned, went round the corner to find Jeff waiting at the phone kiosk, handed the bag over. Jeff tied it to his satchels and manoeuvred the bike across the traffic. Into the alleyway by the Community Centre and through the flats. Then out on the Kennington Road, he shifted the bike into top gear and moved like Meatloaf's bat. Ben had carried on walking and as he reached The Cricketers pub, a van pulled up, two blacks hustled him into the back. Nobody paid any attention. At 8.10am Jeff arrived at Lambeth North Station. I was waiting outside. I asked, 'Okay?'

He was sweating and smiling, 'No prob.'

I took the bag and said, 'Later, sweet meat.'

Into the station, I took the Bakerloo line to the Elephant and Castle. There I caught the Morden train, moving fast. The rhythm in my body urging *go, go, go,* and my mind scoffing, Fuck 'em if they can't take a joke.

8.55am, I was back in my room, money strewn across the bed and sweat teeming down my body, said:

'Piece o' cake really.'

I was into adrenaline overpeak and that shot my lithium level perilously close to toxic. Had to climb on down. I lay on the bed and began a slow backward count 100... 99... 98...

Knock on the door.

Jesus, my heart shot through the roof of my mouth. On to me already.

Asked, 'Who is it?'

Thinking, Where's the bloody bat? and wishing I had something with pump action.

'You wish for me to make the bed?'

Near hysterical, I answered, 'No... no, I've already made my bed.'

Jeez, did I ever! As I heard her move away, I felt a gurgle of suppressed laughter rush through my system and had to bury my face in a towel to hide the sound. Kept thinking, Now all I have to do is lie in it. While I was having a high old time in Clapham, Leon's men were extracting the last of Ben's teeth with a pair of pliers.

Without meaning to, I fell asleep and had me a humdinger of a *chaucon*. What the French call a dream. See, them languages just drip offa me.

I was on a bike and trying to out-pedal some hound of heaven in malevolent pursuit. Lithium was strapped to the handlebars but I couldn't stop to take it. Jeff was ahead with a bundle of *Big Issues* screaming, 'I can't sell this!'

Alongside was Jack waving those driving gloves at me and singing, 'Bye-Bye, Brady.' Roz featured too and kept calling me 'QUEER.' If I could get off the bike, I'd kill her, I knew I would. But, the hound was right up close. My own shout woke me, I said, 'Jesus.'

Disorientated, I couldn't understand what I was lying on. Crawled off the bed and bundles of money came with me, I said, 'What the fuck...?'

Then I realised and instead of celebration, I got a real bad feeling, muttered, 'The Hackman blues.'

Got into the shower and scalded the skin right into my bones. I felt so old and said, 'Yo' buddy, you are old.'

As I shaved, I noticed the lines in my face were etched deep. You could plant spuds in them. Some people, their faces... so lined and you hear the expression – 'lived-in face.'

Mine had been squatted in and for too long. Eviction was way overdue. Some rents can't be paid. I knew that.

It was evening, I'd slept the whole day. A tap on the door and Spiro entered carrying a tray. It had a bottle of ouzo and little cheese snacks, he said, 'The mountain come to you my friend.'

I'd tidied the money away, otherwise one of us would have had a coronary. He indicated the snacks, said, 'This is meze, adds bite to the ouzo.'

He poured, then added water. The liquid clouded over, like Pernod or a bad date. He raised his glass, clinked mine, said, '*Yassue*.'

'Whatever.

He slid a snack towards me.

'Sit, eat, Mr Hackman... what a great name but I must confess to liking Mr David Navan.'

'Niven, you mean?'

'Yes, that's who I said.'

'Okay.'

I took a sip of the ouzo... jeez, sheep dip. Farmers sometimes dose sheep with lithium. If a dog kills one of these sheep, he recoils and never again goes near them. Was that the reason dogs gave me a wide berth? Not that I hadn't been with some real dogs in my time.

Oh yeah.

Intuition of the worst kind told me Spiro's story would be long. He looked like a wizened gnome that had been abandoned in an overgrown garden. He was still in the Niven drone, I rejoined the monotone.

'John Mortimer, ah, a true Englishman. I study him, is why I speak so fine.'

He say about Mr Navan's favourite joke. To roar down a ski slope with his manhood bare to the elements. After, he'd push them in brandy to defrost.

I knew the kicker to this. How in one of life's vicious ironies, he'd had to spend the end of his life sitting in a bath of ice hoping it would cure motor neurone disease. Spiro obviously hadn't heard this, so I let it lie. Even Greeks need illusions.

He ate some meze, not a sign of him leaving, then motioned me to drink.

What the hell...

As we feasted, a van pulled up to a make-shift tip at Kennington. Ben's battered body was unceremoniously thrown on to the rubbish. The van accelerated away, then the Minder said, 'Hold on a mo'.' And he jumped out, pushed a copy of the *Big Issue* into Ben's ruined mouth, said, 'You move some copies.'

And they sped off.

Spiro said, 'I think you are a man with some worries.'

Me… I'd ninety-two thousand reasons to be cheerful.

He took a set of beads from his pocket, said, 'These are worry beads. You let them rest in your hand, thread with your fingers and, we say, the beads do the worrying.'

They were black, on a silver chain with a small bright blue stone at the top. He said, 'That is to ward off the evil eye.'

'Could be useful.'

He gave me a direct look, asked, 'How much do you win?'

'Excuse me?'

'From your work.'

'Oh *earn*.'

'Is not the same?'

I gave a tight smile. 'You might have a point, some jobs yes… you could *win* a stack.'

The Greeks have a directness bordering on bluntness. I'd like to say it's refreshing but it ain't. Now he changed tack.

'You are a married man?'

'Absolutely. Roz, my missus, is – alas – detained at the moment.'

'*Ti krima.*' (What a pity.)

Then: 'I like the cinema, I read Hollywood magazines so much. I know many things.'

A Greek Barry Norman and almost as modest. Maybe time to get his attention, like Mr Magoo, to get him focused.

I said, 'I have a story you might not know.'

He popped an olive in his mouth, its black skin taut against his teeth as he gave a superior smile, a downright smirk, said:

'I believe I know all the stories.'

'Yes, I am sure.'

'Try this: Foreman, the film director took Romy Schneider's son to a tennis match. But, he left the boy to make his own way home. The boy was only ten. At his grandmother's house he tried to climb through a window but he slipped…'

I paused for a touch of ouzo. Spiro looked suitably sick.

'…And was impaled on a spike. A passer-by removed it in an attempt to help and the boy bled to death. A year later Romy Schneider committed suicide.'

Spiro seemed like he'd gone into a trance. I touched my glass to his…

Clink!

… and said, 'But I guess you already heard it… yeah?'

He looked at his watch, said:

'Christos! I must to the desk.'

'Drop us in the paper, would you?'

A few moments later, the *Standard* was pushed under the door. I reckoned that would fix Spiro's visits. That story comes from my post mania periods, when the depression locks on images and thoughts of death like a vice. I was glad to have shared. How often do you get to drop a nugget like that into everyday conversation? It's a show-stopper.

Settled back to read the paper. It had Barbara Cartland on Oasis. She said:

'A splendid example of young people using talent in a creative way.'

Jaysus, the old bitch was seriously unhinged. I mean, how out of touch can she be?

As immediate response, Liam Gallagher was also quoted. He gallantly said:

'Women have had me over. After I've bopped them, they've gone and sold it to the papers. Fair play. But I've just come in their gob and gone off, so therefore I've had them over. Tied one-all baby.'

The hetero in all his strutting glory. I threw the paper aside, said, 'Enough of this shit.'

Bundled all the money into the hold-all, had to push it hard. The ouzo was coursing through me, I felt almost like I do at the onset of mania. To add folly to recklessness, I double chugged hefty shots of caffeine, belched and said, 'Wow.'

I walked to Victoria in near record time. An energy burning in me couldn't wait for a bus or even a cab. Down at the Oval I passed a wino, renowned for his foul tongue. He regularly chants a stream of invective at passers-by and makes damn sure it's personal. A while back he'd launched a tirade at me. Most people, most times, ignore him. Not me.

I walked straight over and gave him two large whacks to the side of his head. He cried:

'I'm sorry… I didn't mean it, I'm sorry!'

'Yeah, you're sorry now all right.'

He was appropriately silent as I cruised by.

At the time I was doing 600 mgs of lithium daily.

When I got to Victoria railway station, the levels were indeed rising. I felt a sense of disorientation descend but managed to get a left-luggage locker and bung the holdall in. I could barely extract the key as my whole body began to tremble.

As I turned, I walked into the row of lockers opposite. For all appearances, I looked like the wino I'd silenced.

A cop approached…

'Are you all right sir?'

I collapsed and an ambulance was called. In my wallet there's a note describing my condition, so they could tell how perilously toxic I was. An intravenous drip was applied and I was effectively off the board. For the next two days I remained at the hospital. A vital time with the various players. The day of my discharge I was sitting in a wheelchair, almost dozing. Not that I needed either the chair or the sleep but they like to see you off the premises in a submissive state.

I heard, 'Evening all,' and snapped awake.

Chief Inspector Nolan, without his sidekick. He was wearing a spectacular blue suit, one that would make even John Travolta pause. He asked, 'Like the suit?'

'I'm dazzled, truly am.'

'The missus picked it out… it was remaindered at John Lewis.'

'Can't think why.'

He had a brown paper bag in his hands, clutched tight. Now he looked up and down the corridor, asked, 'Any chance of a cuppa? I'm gasping.'

'No.. they've been.

'Shite… but how remiss of me. Here I am, prattling away about me and I never asked about you. I was flipping through the log when I came across your name… Hello, I said, what's this then?… Taken poorly, were we?'

Little did he realise just how poorly. If it had been a few minutes earlier, I wouldn't have made that locker and… yeah, that would have been all she wrote.

I said:

'I'm okay now.'

'But I, alas, have not received my stipend… am I being dropped? The missus and I have come to rely, nay cherish the little things, those foolish luxuries… like meat!'

'An oversight, I'll get right on it.'

'Would you? How kind, how downright spiffing. For an arse-bandit, you have such consideration.'

The doctor came and Nolan moved. Not far but out of earshot.

The doctor said, 'I'd like you to come back in for some blood tests and there are a few other items I'd like to screen. I'm a tad concerned about some marks…'

'I was run over by a bike and a thug.'

'…As soon as possible.'

'I'll do that.'

Thinking… In yer dreams pal. I'm Stateside.

He repeated his admonitions and left.

Nolan strolled back, said, 'What's up doc?'

'Jeez, how original!'

He offered the brown bag, saying 'The missus sent these. Notice my affection for her. None of that bar-room boy shit about 'er indoors.

I opened the bag. There were six black grapes.

I said, 'Jeez, you're a prince! Sure ye can afford it, I don't want to leave the household short?'

He gave a spectacular grin that lit up the suit and maybe even the corridor, said:

'Fair cop guv, I put up my mitt, I nibbled.'

I slung them in the litter basket, said:

'You shouldn't have gone to any trouble.'

'Trouble? Oh, it wasn't any trouble. If it had been that, I'd have sent my sergeant… then you'd know what the fucking word means.'

He spun on his heel and left. A porter wheeled me to the door and I asked, 'Can you call me a cab?'

'Naw, sorry mate, not in my contract.'

I thought, Maybe it's because I'm a Londoner… and hummed the rest as I eased into the real world. I'd have sung the 'Lambeth Walk' but I can never remember the words.

19

The headline:

BIG ISSUE VENDOR MURDERED

With a sick heart, I bought the paper. It detailed the discovery of Ben's body and its condition. The police were treating it as a squabble over gang territory. The thought occurred that Ben would never get to read Jimmy J now.

Took the tube to Clapham and eyeballed everybody. I didn't know if my two day hiatus had helped or hindered me. I do know I was flaming paranoid.

When I got to the hotel, Spiro was in a high old state.

'Mr Hackman, Mr Hackman, I am so concerned.'

'What? thought I'd skipped it did you... done a runner eh?'

He was offended.

'Of course no – *ohi*... I was worried.'

'You have beads for that sort of thing, don't you?'

And left him to it.

In the room, I showered and tried to ease my thundering heart. Dressed in old cords, sweatshirt, trainers and Levi jacket. Battle fatigues. Took the bat and put it in a Gap socks bag. Then on to the phone... No answer from Balham... Jesus... then Jeff. He answered on first ring.

I said shrewdly, 'Jeff.'

'Oh Tony... oh God Almighty... did you see the papers? That bloke from the Oval... and then I thought they'd killed you... I...'

He launched into a frenzied babble and I had to roar:

'JEFF!'

No doubt they heard me in Balham. 'Calm the fuck down, it's okay...'

'But Tony... black men have been asking at the courier office... I...'

'SHUT UP!'

He did and I said quietly, 'Take some things and get out. Check into The Coburg Hotel in Bayswater.'

'Why there?'

'Cos it's outa south-east London, cos I can reach you there... cos I SAY SO!'

'All right Tony, I will... I'll do that... that's what I'll do. Should I take my scripts?'

'Jesus... yeah... take them.. I'll talk to you later.'

'What's happening Tony?'

'Fucked if I know'

And I rung off. Had to sit for a moment, I was still fragile from the hospital. I needed a holiday not a war.

Called a cab and passed a silent Spiro on the way. I had this effect on people. The cabbie was a Rasta and the smell of weed was pungent.

He asked, 'Wanna tote, mon?'

'No Balham, actually.'

'Dat cool, I like Balham.'

His radio was on and... no, not Bob Marley... that golden oldie again. Long John Baldry with 'Let The Heartache Begin.'

Could he sing or what? Like Simon and Garfunkel in 'The Boxer', I took some comfort there.

We took the slow scenic route, managed to miss every green light and aggravated every motorist en route. He was oblivious to it all. When we got there, I paid and asked, 'Wanna tip?'

'Sure, mon.'

'Mellow out, you're too uptight.'

At the door to the warehouse I took a deep breath and

pushed it open. Reed was sitting in the middle of the room, a sawn-off resting on his knees. No sign of anybody else. He said

'Dee man.'

'Are you okay?'

'I look okay?'

'Yeah.'

'Then I be okay'.

The shotgun didn't change position, aimed at my groin.

I said, 'You wanna move that, Reed?'

'Yo' tink I shoots yo'?'

'Jeez, I hope not. Where's Danny and the girl?'

'They run off, yo' run off… it contagious.'

'I was sick.'

'Dat disease bro', I gots it too.'

'What?'

'Yeah, yo' be a maniac an' it depresses me.'

I pulled up a chair, said, 'Fuck, what a shambles.'

'I don' told you… but yo' don listen.'

'Where could they have gone?'

'You gets dee money?'

'Yeah, I…'

'Gimme my cut.'

'If that's what you want but on an educational note, it's not called "manic depression" anymore.'

'What yo' say?'

'It's now termed Bipolar Disorder – *bi* as in both… geddit? A person suffers from both mania and depression, not just depression on its tod.'

Reed gave me the look, said:

'Yeah, as in bi-zarre and dat you, dude!'

I explained that the money was in a locker at Victoria and he said:

'So, git goin', what cha all be standing here fo'.'

'What will you do, with the money, I mean?'

'I goes back to mah roots.'

'To Brixton?'

He gave the old familiar sigh, 'To Ethiopia, where Haile Selassie be.'

'Oh.'

If he'd volunteered to come with me, maybe I'd have given him half the contents of the lot, half of the ninety-two. But seeing as he didn't know Jack had paid up… tough titty. I made a final effort, asked,

'Shouldn't we try and find Danny? Maybe roll the dice one more time, grab the girl again?'

He laughed out loud.

'Make it a weekly thang, go grab de bitch every Friday… yo' mo' than crazy bro', yo' all a sick person and I's got to git de hell away.'

So I legged it off to Victoria, took the bag into the public toilets at the station and carefully counted out his cut. Skimmed a few large off his end to account for attitude. Then put the bag back in the locker.

When I returned, it didn't seem as if he'd moved from the chair, but at least the sawn-off was pointed downward, like our plans.

I said:

'Wanna count it?'

'No.'

'You trust me?'

'No… but if yo' be cheating me, what I gonna do… shoot yo?'

I put out my hand said, 'I guess it's sayonara.'

'Say what?'

'Goodbye, Reed.'

He stood up and there was a moment. As if we'd hug maybe. It hung there like severity, then leaked away.

He moved to the door, said, 'It don' mean nuttin', drive on.'

I dunno what I felt when I was alone. No man had ever been closer to me or helped me more and what did it come down to? At the end it meant a sawn-off measuring the distance between us. I said aloud to the emptiness, 'I'll miss you bro'.'

Like so many other things, the timing was just a little off.

FUNERAL : OF THE WINO

Blame it on
an intuition
I hadn't heard
and certainly
would nigh on
absolutely know,
a life upon the streets
at least for long
I'd not survive
the sabotage in hope.

For far too long
I'd lived
a lithium above despair
a hearse before
I watched the homeless
place their hand
above their heart and knew
if they had hats
would slow and very slow remove
the trembling notwithstanding
a silence in respect.

The cortege press
his hand the crowds across
this moment new
passed nigh beyond
the oldest explanation
a hand towards
expectations
not renewed

The coffin doesn't pass
the rich hotels
that cater to
the very rich... exclusively
their hands
towards the exhortations
aren't shaped
as if they ever were.

– Grace B

20

There were violent clashes in Brixton the nights before Ben's funeral. The second night a huge police presence lost it and lobbed CS canisters. The crowd surged back and the front page of the papers showed a Rasta astride a police horse, dreadlocks streaming, a fist in the air, to the caption:

BRIXTON BURNS

Does it ever.

Leon, as a leading figure in the community, had appealed for calm and he had volunteered to walk behind the hearse.

A nod's as good as a wink... if he was doing that... who was minding the club?

Course, I know. I know I should have said, 'To hell with it all,' taken the money and run. But I'd liked Ben and I'd given him my word and not kept it. If nothing else, I owed, if not to the bigger picture, at least to the *Big Issue*.

The day of Reed's departure, I headed to Bayswater. Jeez, what a calm place. Nobody speaks English and maybe that helps. I checked into The Coburg and ordered a bottle of Old Tennessee. I'd some calls to make.

Jack first... he came on the line in Hackman mould, full of fire and ferocity, demanded:

'Where the hell have you been, mister?'

'No hello?'

'Don't be impertinent, you know what that brings.'

'Gee, I'm nervous now. Anyway, I gave the cash to Leon.'

'So where's my girl.'

'Leon said… hold on a sec Jacko, I had to write it down, no wonder help is at such a premium… oh yeah, here it is…'

And I waited. I was remembering how I felt when the thug bounced me off the dashboard.

He shouted, 'Well, get on with it.'

'Oh, you want me to read it… okay, so… he said: "Go fuck your white ass."'

More silence, so I added, 'Anyway, he's busy with the funeral for Benjamin, he'll be walking behind the hearse. I think Roz will stay home, service the other blacks.'

The hate channelled down the wire and I actually held the receiver at arm's length. You can get too close.

He said: 'You better run, boyo, run fast and far.'

'Why?'

'I'll be talking to you, Mr Brady, right up close.'

'Promise?'

And he slammed the phone down.

Next I got the desk to connect me to Jeff's room.

'Tony, is it you?'

'Alive and shaking.'

'Oh God, I'm running up a bill here Tony.'

'Let it run sweetcakes, my mate Reed's picking up the tab.'

'Who?'

'Nobody, not no more, he's gone to the mountain seeking the prophet.'

'When will I see you?'

'How would five minutes be? I'm on the top floor.'

'I'm on my way.'

I had intended getting a pair of those Calvin Klein briefs, be on the bed with them on and a rose between my teeth.

Room Service came and I tipped freely. Opened the bottle and smelt it… ah, poured and sipped. Tasted like the good times that hadn't yet rolled. A tap on the door and there was Jeff.

I said, 'Wotcha waiting for? Drop them jeans.'

He did.

I wish I could say it was sublime. That when emotion got added to sex, you got Nirvana.

Naw.

What it was, was energetic and sweaty and brief. He was disappointed. I suppose if you've been cooped up in a room, terrified and bewildered, a wham-bam is somewhat less than enchanting.

He said, 'You're not big on foreplay.'

'No, I like to get to the main event, punch in, hit the canvas.'

I poured the Old Number 7, clinked his glass, he knocked it back like a fish hand.

I said, 'Aw shit, it's sipping whiskey... you got to smell and savour, let it tease yer tastebuds.'

He rounded on me, 'I don't believe it... you want foreplay with a bottle but not with a person. That's very sad.'

'Jeez Jeff, don't get deep on me... c'mon.'

Can a man pout? Jeff sure tried and being an actor, it came easily.

He said: 'I've been so worried.'

I got off the bed, rummaged in my clothes, said, 'I'm glad you said that, I've got just the thing for you.'

And handed him the worry beads. I then gave the Spiro spiel and embellished a bit. The bottom line emphasising the trouble I'd gone to procure it. His face wasn't lit up and I figured I'd told it badly, asked, 'You don't like it?'

'I got one on Míkonos last year.'

I snapped it back, growled, 'Fuck, sorry to be predictable.'

He moved over to me, asked, 'What happens from here, can I return to my flat?'

'How'd you like to go to San Francisco, like tomorrow, how'd that be?'

'I have an audition in a few days, a part in *Eastenders*.'

My plans were sliding down the toilet.

I said, 'Jeff, you can't go back to yer life yet. Gimme a couple of days to sort out things, wait for me in America and we'll have a ball, hell we'll even have foreplay.'

He stood up, said in a prissy voice, 'I don't think so. We do have a police force to deal with this sort of stuff. I can't jeopardise my career and – loathe though I am to say it – I don't think we're compatible.'

I grabbed him by the back of the neck, whispering, 'This is real life, son. There's people out there who'll do untold damage to you and they like doing it. I'm trying to help you, for fuck's sake.' And I let him go.

He was white with fear and/or anger… bi-agitated, in fact.

Drew his body up in that English way. You kick the living crap outa them but they'll have the last bloody word. Always sound as if they're terminating an interview and you didn't get the job. He said:

'I see. Well Tony, I'll be leaving now. I won't say I'm not disappointed, I had hoped that…'

'Can it buddy, okay?'

'I beg your pardon, I'm not finished.'

Now it's my turn to get English, said, 'You didn't by any chance write a letter for Danny's dad, did you? Don't beg any frigging pardons with me. I HATE THAT SHIT! See, I'm shouting now. You actors are all the same, one shag and you're history. Go on then, fuck off.'

He did. I stood for a few moments, deep breathing and struggling for control, muttering, 'I'm okay… yeah… loosen them muscles… yeah… I'm creator of my own life… I have a right to be here!'

Stood a second, let the serenity settle – then I punched a hole in the wall.

Outside The Coburg a guy asked me for change. I gave him the worry beads, he asked, 'What's this shite?'

'My question exactly.'

I was going to need a gun. Only one place I knew was stocking them and that was Danny's place. But it meant I'd have to see Crystal.

What was I going to tell her? That Danny was in lust and had buggered off with a young woman with a degree. Yeah, she was going to love that.

But I couldn't go to Brixton with just a bus pass. The bat wouldn't be quite the speed when I actually went ballistic. I thought of my derailed plans for Jeff. How I'd wanted to re-enact the part of Maupin's 'Tales' where the guy raves about weejuns. If there's a more comfortable pair of shoes, I hadn't heard of them.

Took a cab to Danny's place and I was nervous. Stood outside and willed myself to ring the door. Did… and no reply. The relief was enormous. I put on that bemused look, so beloved of Neighbourhood Watch watchers everywhere. I didn't scratch my head but gave the impression. Started the dance of looking up at the windows the – 'Gee, someone should be home.' Then the slide round the side of the house. Again, the looking round and whacked my elbow into a window. No alarms unless it was one of those silent jobs, in which case I was fucked. Put my hand through and opened the frame wide. How fast would the cops come to a burglar's home… yeah, he'd not be top priority. The smell hit me straight away. In my very worst moments of depression, it had lived in my nostrils…

The smell of death.

She was hanging from the light-chord in the bedroom. From the bruises on her face she'd been beaten first. Dressed in an old nightie, there was a sock on one foot… Mickey Mouse. I wanted to throw up but kept control.

I whispered, 'Oh Crystal… oh God, I'm so sorry.'

I didn't cut her down. I didn't want my prints there and resolved to wipe what I'd already touched. Took me twenty minutes to find the weapons in a cubby hole in the airing-cupboard. Selected a mess of stuff, all lethal. Lifted up the bottom of the hidey-hole and found nearly three grand. Took that too. On my way out I deliberately didn't look at her. An overwhelming desire to touch her hand came over me but I fought it. Wiped down everything I'd touched and got the hell outa there.

At a brisk pace I headed for The Roebuck and ordered a large scotch. The weapons and money in a laundry bag at my feet. I felt hollow. A barmaid said, 'You look like you've seen a ghost.' 'Me? no… no, I haven't seen a thing.' Like the Neighbourhood Watch in fact.

21

Rented a car from the outfit 'who care more'. They didn't seem to give much of a toss to me but hey, I wasn't in a responsive mood. I'd wanted an Audi but going into Brixton…? And if things went well, coming out I'd need a tank, Settled on a VW Golf, cos it accelerates on suspense and you can park it anywhere, space isn't a problem. When I said I'd pay cash, her look said:

Drug Dealer.

I said:

'Sorry to insult you with money. Blame my upbringing. We were taught you had to pay for things… stupid eh?'

Next up was Cohen's off the Charing Cross Road. Any outfit you want, they'll fit you up. Even Village People would be pleased. When I said what I wanted, the guy never blinked an eye, so I added, 'Will you be offended by cash?'

'I like being offended.'

My kind of people.

Drove carefully back to Clapham, as Kevin Kline said in *The Untouchables*: 'Careful as mice at a crossroad.'

I'd soon see who was touchable.

Next morning, the day of Ben's funeral, I get my gear together and drove over to Balham. I half-expected, half-hoped to find Reed there. But it was deserted. I brewed some coffee and selected my hardware. There was a twelve gauge pump, the barrel sawn down. Yeah, I could bring that. I'd put the Glock in my waist-band . So light it could have been a toy. Made of shiny black plastic, it fits designer-tight. The terrorists' weapon of choice as it goes, undetectable by metal scanners. Thirdly, I'd put a Browning automatic in the pocket of my jacket.

As I had a second coffee, I loaded all three and accustomed myself to the feel. They felt like bad news. A thick coating of black tape was wrapped round the handle of the Browning. It fit like a glove. Now here was an item that had seen active service and it was gonna see more.

I turned on the radio, got the local bulletins. The police were asking that people stay away from Brixton unless they had legitimate business. Church leaders appealed for calm. The Left asked for support, to show solidarity with the homeless.

It was shaping up. I'd taken my lithium and now I was just taking my time. At the end of the warehouse, under boxes of pottery, Reed kept a stash. Checked and it was still there. I did some lines of coke and smoked a little weed. Blending me a mental cocktail that was already getting a fizz. A rush from the coke that could have been clarity but was too fleeting to analyse.

Roy Orbison came on with that Elvis Costello song and I nodded... Yeah, comedians was bloody right... have I got a joke today, guys?

Then, time to get dressed. Put the costume on and thought, Okay baby.

Distributed the weapons around my body and put the pump in a Tesco bag. I was the American Dream, sort of:
1. White,
2. Rich-ish,
3. Armed.

Stood on Balham High Road a moment and I swear you could hear the beat of Brixton, Roy Orbison's sound of drums. I considered for a minute what it was the sound carried, then said softly, 'It's the blues.'

Put the Golf in gear, pulled out carefully, heading for home. The Golf had a tape-deck and I punched in one of my favourites. Snatches and pieces I'd recorded over the years. Works for me. Lindisfarne with 'Run For Home', but I fast forwarded. Forever ruined by Gazza. If you want to hear hell on vinyl, hear that. Ideally he should duet with Imelda Marcos on 'Feelings' and you'd understand the term, Desert Storm.

Next up was Tori Amos with 'Me and a Gun'. Serendipity or what? Eat yer rain forest, Sting. Tori sure catches the essence of mania in full flight. I didn't sing along but gave intermittent shouts of, 'Yeah' and, 'Too bloody right.'

I wondered how Ben would have felt now that *he'd* become the Big Issue – from vendor to essence.

A police check-point at the very entrance to Brixton. Time to test the costume. A young copper holding a clipboard motioned me to roll down the window, his eyes locked on my neck and he said, 'Sorry Vicar, we have to ensure the legitimacy of each vehicle.'

'You do great work my son, my flock will sorely need me this day.'

'Go right on through. I'll put the PASS sticker on your windscreen.'

'God bless you, son.'

And drove on. In fact, I felt a little holy. Drugs will do that to you every time.

The funeral was already halted and a stand-off had begun. Riot police fingered their batons and the crowd taunted. I knew it wouldn't be too long 'til they got down and played the Brixton boogie. I parked near the top of Electric Avenue. Brixton has all sorts of moods but of all the guises it wears, dullness ain't among them.

Dirty
Dangerous
Vibrant
Degenerate
Exciting
Unexpected.

Yeah! And now it was actually humming. The TV stations already hustling for strategic position, they'd smelt the blood in the water. Morley's had a pre-riot sale as they knew that everything would definitely go – including the windows.

A Rasta with a tea-cosy on his head was flogging T-shirts with the logo:

BEN LIES IN BRIXTON

*****

THE PIGS LIE EVERYWHERE

The scent of joss sticks, weed, incense, danced on the air as militants of every colour set up stalls.

A middle-aged black woman bumped me and asked, 'Reverend, ye gonna bless a po' sinner?'

'You bet sister, go tell it on the mountain.'

It seemed to do her and she pressed a pound coin into my palm. Maybe I'd been in the wrong racket. I held the Tesco bag tightly to my chest and turned away from the crowd. Sweat was running down my spine as I get to the door of the club.

A sign said DELIVERIES ROUND BACK.

That meant me.

As I moved, a huge roar erupted. The hearse was trying to enter the centre and the cops were having none of it. The cup final of civil disturbance had kicked off. All the sides were ready to roll.

The back door was locked and bolted, so I banged heavily. What I'd planned was just getting in there and waiting for Leon, the Minder and whoever. Then we'd see. Like Harrison Ford as Indiana Jones, I'd make it up as I went along. Failing all else, I'd torch it, just one more fire on the Brixton sky-line.

I heard the bolts being drawn back and an irritated muttering. A black man in a string vest threw open the door, saying:

'Dis better be good, bro'.'

'How's this?'

And I clubbed him in the face with the stock of the pump. He went over backwards with a grunt. I moved in and re-bolted the door, then paused... listened. I could hear music and to my astonishment... ABBA!

I was rooted to the spot. In all the scenarios I'd visualised, hearing 'Dancing Queen' never featured. It threw me completely and I'd to do some deep breathing to get in gear.

Silence… then the opening bars of 'Fernando'. Jeez, we could all hear the drums.

A staircase led to the source of the music and I began to climb. I had the pump in both hands and could feel it slick with sweat. Jeez, I thought, what if there's an Abba convention. I could take them all back to Balham.

At the top, I was confronted by an open door, the den, obviously. Leather recliners along the wall, bean bags on the wooden floor. In the middle, dancing, was… Roz, giving it large. She was dressed in a leotard and for such an ugly bitch, she sure moved with pure grace. I pulled the breech to slide a shell into the barrel, squeezed the trigger. The hi-fi exploded and Roz screamed.

I said, 'Thank you for the music.'

She whirled round, spat and said, 'It's the moron again.'

I moved down into the room and picked up the remote. A massive TV was perched near the ruined music centre. I switched on. The rioting was in full hop, so close you could touch it and with the lingering smell of cordite, it was like having it in the room.

I motioned with the gun, said, 'Sit down.'

She didn't, so I added, 'Or I'll knock you down.'

She sat.

If she was scared or even all that surprised, she hid it well. A smirk danced twixt her eyes and her mouth.

She said, 'I can't believe even a cretin like you would be so stupid.'

'Well, there you have it… where's Danny?'

Now she was truly amused, said, 'Why, with his wife of course, save her hanging about.'

She wanted me to know. To know they'd done Crystal. Then the TV commentary got hugely excited.

'A man… a black man behind the hearse has been shot… '

Now I smiled, said, 'Daddy's gone a hunting.'

Her face changed, rage through alarm as she looked at me then back to the screen, shouted, 'What have you done!'

'Me… nothing… but at a guess I'd say sniper.'

'You told my father… Oh, Leon.'

And she leapt at me, nails and teeth clawing. I side-stepped and lashed the side of her head with one of them thug special-ties. She flayed across the floor.

I said, 'The second one hurts even more, can you believe that?'

She rolled on to her side then half sat up, a bruise already forming on her cheek.

Her accent now was pure south-east London, no college control here. All bile.

'Yer friend Danny, he was a poof… yeah, he wanted to try it doggy style… I slit him as he came.'

And pulling open her leotard, she held the plastic cross round her neck, continued…

'To remind me of his pig squealing… and the courier… yer little toy-boy, we lit him up last night.'

I double-actioned the pump and it blew her across the room. I walked over and put two more in. Now the TV was babbling news but I was deafened from the gunfire. I blew the screen apart and pumped the remainder into the couches. Put the gun in the Tesco bag and legged it outa there.

Out on Electric Avenue the riot hadn't over-spilled.

Yet.

I went across the road and stood in the doorway. I sunk down on my knees and was thus, when a black limo screeched down the road. It stopped at the club and a bunch of black men poured out. I distinctly saw Leon, live as hate.

AFTER
GLOW

22

I did what any self respecting gay manic depressive would do.
I ran like fuck.

I spent that night in a numb state at the hotel. Everything had got away from me. I didn't know how to rein it in or if I even wanted to.

Jeff
Ben
Roz
Danny
Crystal
ALL DEAD.

A line from Flaubert burned in my head:

'I'm crammed with coffins, like an old cemetery.'

Reed was MIA… I was lithium leaded.

Next day, I bundled my gear together and paid the bill. In an attempt at levity, Spiro said:

'Your wife will be happy for your return.'

I snapped, 'Wise up.'

As I went he said, '*Kalo taxidi.*'

I figured he wished wrath of cab drivers on me or some such drivel. When I learnt a bit of Greek later, I found it was, 'good journey.' Yeah, like that.

Rented a long-stay locker and stashed the guns, the bat, most of the money. Next I went to Earl's Court and into a late departures agency, booked the early morning flight to Athens. Not because I felt that's where I wanted to go, but it was the first available. Then to Marks and Spencer for some lightweight clothes.

Keep it simple:

Two jeans

T-Shirts

Moccasins.

I didn't venture near my house. I let the landlord repossess, I couldn't give a toss. Had my lithium supplies restocked and I was ready to roll. The flight was scheduled for 2am, so I had 'till midnight. Checked into one of those back-packer places near Abingdon Road and laid low.

I had only one call to make before I had to head for Gatwick. I rang him. As always, he picked up on the first ring.

'Yeah?'

'Hello, Jack.'

'Brady… I hope you found a deep rat hole to hide in.'

'I've get to hand it to you Jack, you sure fucked it up.'

'Me?'

'Your sniper… he shot the wrong man. What's the problem, they all look alike to him?'

'There'll be other times.'

'Not for Roz.'

'What?'

'Leon took her out – retribution he calls it.'

'Oh Jesus… oh God… '

'Oh, and I figured something else too… she wasn't just yer daughter was she… ? She was yer wife… at least "wife" in the biblical sense.'

'How dare you?'

'I saw *Chinatown*. All that Hackman… a bloody snow job. I was looking at the wrong movie. Well here's one for you to rent – Hackman in *The Hunting Party*. At least *he* could shoot.'

I thought I could hear sobbing and I said, 'I'm going to be out of the picture for a bit but no worries, I'll be back… it'll be like a sequel. Bye, Jack.'

I bought a pack of cigarettes. The battle to stop had been awesome but hey… *click*… I was a smoker again. The first few pulls and I dizzied out but that's why we came.

Decided to go the full route and bought a Zippo. That solid clunk when you close it, it sounds like significance. I bought it secondhand from one of those stalls off Kensington High Street. The traders are Russian and Lithuanian or shit… I dunno, maybe even Lutheran. The look they have, they've seen it all.

On the side of the lighter it said, '52nd Airborne' and that seemed about right, considering the source.

I liked it.

Michael Caine said to Bob Hoskins in *Mona Lisa*: 'It's the little things, George.'

He had a point there.

They say the difference between having a single friend and no-one is immeasurable. Oh yeah, I'll go with that. Or, to really put the boot in:

'No man can be considered a failure who has one friend.'

Well, what can I say? I'd fucked up big time.

At the Departure Lounge at Gatwick, I was examining my duty-free purchase. Carton of cigs and a bottle of Glenfiddich. They didn't have my usual and time it was to let sippin' whisky go. I chose this one cos I liked the name – 'A Glenfiddich please, straight up.' See! You sound like you know yer stuff. In the grand scheme of things, it rates zero but right there, right then, it was a notion to cling to.

As I clung, a bloke came and plonked his self beside me. No by yer leave or anything, just sat on down. He was wearing a crumpled safari suit. There's a place in Jermyn Street they cater to exactly that kind of thing.

You go in, bang down a shit pile of readies and say, 'I want clothes that mark me out as an old India-hand, or old anywhere-hand; that make me look like I was there in the early days. But primarily I want to look like an arse-hole.'

You say that, they fit you out in one of those.

He extended a hand, said gruffly, 'I'm Ross.'

'Painful... is it?'

'Sorry?'

'I've read my Evelyn Waugh.'

'Cheeky blighter.'

Did he mean me or Waugh. He looked at my purchases then asked, 'Might I give you a tip?'

'If you have to.'

'Skip Athens – it's too much for a first timer. Go straight to the islands, get acclimatised.'

'How d'ya know it's my first time?'

He gave a patient smile, said, 'You bought cigarettes.'

'That's not on?'

'Cheaper in Greece, all your internationals, cheaper than duty free.'

'Oh.'

'How'd you like to be a New Warrior?'

I laughed out loud. Jeez, you'd have to.

He wasn't fazed and continued, 'There's too much feminisation of modern man. Our virility is being eroded but now, we're taking it back.'

He was in full mouth and I had to block, said:

'Iron John lives, yeah.'

'You read that! Splendid... truly capital. You are already initiated.'

'Whoa, Toss.'

'Ross actually.'

'Whoever. Hold the phone, I heard of it... okay... I didn't read it.'

'No problems, as we warriors say. We're having a three day fest on the Island of Kíthnos for a select band of twenty candidates.'

'Fest?'

'We live off the land in a ragged terrain. Only our wits and abilities to sustain us. It's a cleansing... a return to our ordained nature.'

'Jesus!'

'I like you sir, you have fettle.'

'Listen Doss, I grew up in Brixton... how much more of a warrior could I be?'

'You'll like us... pick up the standard... rally to our cry.'

'Jeez, keep your voice down. I do like a man, a pick-up's even better... and this is free... is it?'

Conspiratorial look as he bent his head in low. An overwhelming urge to give him a big wallop to the side of his head but contained it,

He said quietly, 'Alas, there are some minor expenses.'

'How minor?'

'All told, including literature and tapes, four hundred.'

He said that in a rush. As if a fast figure would appear a low one.

I said:

'FOUR HUNDRED? You think you saw me coming... that it?'

The boarding call was announced and I stood up.

I said, 'Abba had a Brixton moment... did you know that... ? Yeah... so *voulez vous couchez avec mel*. You want to feel a man... cop that.'

And I jerked my groin at him.

He was up and gone like a true warrior. I thought he wouldn't last a spit on a slow night at The Fridge. Jeez, I hoped the rioters hadn't torched that.

As I walked down the aisle of the plane, I had to pass him but he buried his head in the safety instructions. Possibly made aviation history by voluntarily reading them.

I got a window seat and stared out at the tarmac. Gee, it was interesting. Rain fell and that added variety. A little later we got airborne and I shuffled round in the cramped space to get comfortable.

Blew my nose. A fucking cold was all I needed...

23

As the plane levelled out from its ascent, I swear I could see the fires of Brixton still burning. Throwing a glow across the London skyline and a shadow across my life. I knew it's fancy and the angle of ascent ruled out such a view. But the flames of the city would always smoulder in my heart.

If you've no-one left to miss, then perhaps you best miss a place. Already I was pining for the midden that is London. So okay... it's a city on its knees and plagued by all the modern pestilences but there was no place I would rather be... or had ever been.

I was fingering the Zippo and feeling all this loss, when the stewardess came marching down, said, 'We have a strict policy of no smoking on this airline.'

'I wasn't about to.'

She gave me the look says, 'pull the other one', and I added, 'I think I'm going to like you a lot.'

She harrumphed and went off to do airline things. I didn't think she'd be offering me tips on what to do and see in Greece. She didn't.

My head was split with a pain that only London flu can devise. I was shredding Kleenex like a woman in a commercial.

Getting off the plane in Athens, I walked into a blanket of heat. It bounced up off the tarmac like a warning. Inside the terminal, I was shooed through customs, fast, furious and unpopular.

I changed a bundle of money and walked outside, said, 'Flu or not, here I come.'

I had the means, I certainly had the inclination, so to begin I was going first class. Hailed a yellow cab and said, 'Hotel Grande Bretagne.'

The driver perked up as if electrified and we burnt rubber outa there. No Smoking signs in various languages littered the upholstery. He chain-smoked some foul tobacco. I lit up myself and felt it bounce off my heart. It didn't help my cold any.

His radio was at Brixton level and it attacked a wall of sound that swept in through his open window. A string of worry beads hung from the mirror and I concentrated on not looking at them. The sound was like chaos and I understood that. I'd lived in it and with it all my life.

No shit, the hotel was grand and then some. I had a balcony overlooking Syntagma Square. I finally got to know what the word opulence meant and the place was reeking in it. The bell-boy, who was about my age, told me that Winston Churchill had been nearly assassinated there. I figured they'd do me in with the bill.

The first thing I did was sleep and the nightmares came calling, a mix of Jeff selling the *Big Issue*, tied to a burning stake and Roz as the twelve-gauge took her apart. Drenched in sweat, I woke with a scream, stumbled out on to the balcony to grab some polluted air. You know how it goes, you see somebody without much awareness and then they keep popping up 'til you finally ask, like the Sundance Kid, 'Who are those guys?'

At Gatwick two bald blokes had been debating the merits of red versus white wine. They were so alike, they had to be brothers. It seemed odd to me you'd hang with a bald brother, when you were like an egg too... much less go on holiday with him. But, what did I know, maybe they were proud of their scalps?

Now, there they were again in Palace jerseys and shorts right beneath my balcony. I wanted to shout, 'Baldies... how goes it?'

But then what?

Yeah.

I got a map from reception, sneaked a look at the tariff and shuddered. One night would be my lot, else I'd have to snatch a Greek. Headed for Plaka, the touts waylaid me at every step. My plans for my stay were simple:

1. Get laid a lot
2. Get brown
3. Get bearded
4. Get resolved
5. Lose the cold

The fourth I needed to do in order to allow me to go back to London and do the business. After fumbling round for an hour, I hailed a cab and asked, 'Where's the best gay club?'

I figured, How offended could he be? These guys kicked the whole shindig into play.

He wasn't offended at all.

Took me to the posh area and pulled up outside. The Alexander Club, whatever else, looked busy. Inside it was sleazy but I wasn't complaining. Sleaze I could handle. Picked up an Aussie back-packer and gave him a fast one in the toilet. Said, as I came, 'Now that's down-under dinkum,' and cursed my running nose.

Next day I booked into a cheap hotel and discovered that mosquitoes are a common nuisance. Over the next few days I saw:

The Acropolis
The Agora
The Thesen
Hadrian's Arch
Temple of Zeus
National Museum
Changing of the Guard

...and it bored me shitless. If this was culture, give me Brixton on a bad-ass Saturday night.

I took a boat to Míkonos and loved that. Over twelve hours and the combination of sea and sun just lulled me into near-lithium peace. My beard had started and already my skin was burning. I bought a pair of steel rimmed plain sunglasses and resembled a nazi on vacation. I was doing okay. I liked the brand name – Police.

Getting off the boat at Míkonos, I heard 'Tank' by T-Rex. I wish it weren't true, I mean how auspicious a landing can it be? I wish too I didn't remember the song so clearly and worse, remember the poster.

Yeah.

Marc Bolan in all his glitter with a toy tank between his legs. I kid you not. Marc himself looked like a badly fucked leprechaun. As I walked off the gangplank, I saw Bald Inc at a café. It has to be said, those domes were tanning, and uniformly.

One of them turned and waved!

The paranoia get up on its hind legs and brayed, 'They're following you.'

My nose began to run.

I'd had this unshakeable flu for for six days now… More? A London-bought course of antibiotics had no effect. In fact, it was getting worse.

Lugging my hold-all, humming T-Rex – not an easy accomplishment – I walked right up to the baldies, asked:

'You following me?'

They were dressed in the Palace singlets and shorts, with thongs on their feet. A cool carafe of orange juice lay before them. One said:

'You what?'

'You heard.'

'Jeez mate, look at the facts… We were here before you. Be an odd way to follow a bloke.'

The other said:

'You've get a nasty cold there, son. Take a pew, have some OJ… London, ain't cha?'

Their own vowels were steeped in the accent you only find south of the river – and what a comfort.

I sat.

Ever since I'd left London, I'd felt tired. Delayed shock, I figured. Close up, the two weren't alike at all. One held out his hand, said, 'I'm Bob, this here's me mate, Rodney.'

I said, 'I'm Tony, I thought you were brothers.'

Big laugh from the boys.

'Naw, never happened, it's what people always fink…'

He looked round, added, 'Though in this bleeding place, they fink we're a couple of poofters.'

We all had a chuckle at this. The very idea...

Bob asked, 'You get stuck with this place too, eh...? Last minute booking at Cosmos... right?'

What could I say?

I said, 'Right.'

Then for deflection asked, 'What's with the Kojaks?'

'It's the fashion mate.'

'Yeah, if yer in yer twenties.'

'Didn't you see Daniel Benzali in *Murder One*?'

'What, the bookshop?'

'Series mate, twenty-six episodes, Bloody cracker it was, we got it on vid.'

'Oh.'

I stood up, said: 'Well, see you guys later, I'd better go check in.'

'You do that mate, 'n' if anyone drops some coins, don't bend over... know what I mean...? Nudge, nudge.'

Yeah, I knew what he meant.

I stayed at... wait for it... The Míkonos.

You got to wonder how they thought of that one. Next few days I did nowt but sun-bathe and sleep. I was in gay paradise and my libido had dropped to ground zero.

Now my throat hurt and I'd developed chest pains, said, 'Age is a bastard.'

Shaved my skull... why not? I might not be well, but at least I could be current. The flu persisted. People praise Greece for its history, islands, yogurt... Me, I rate its chemists. You go in, a geezer speaks English and you ask for anything and it's yours. You go in Boots and ask for aspirin, they grill you like Special Branch and you're lucky to get two pills. On Míkonos I got anti-biotics and thought, Second dose, we'll shift this sucker fast.

Into the next week and I was brown... and bald... and gorgeous. Well... okay I was tanned and it makes you appear healthy. My weight was dropping too and I felt that had to be good. If only I wasn't so knackered all the time.

I'd lie on the beach all day, swear I'd hit the nightlife later... and be in bed, alone, at seven and worse... glad of it.

Had I leapt into old age? Just skipped out on late middle-age and fallen fucked into decrepitude? That's how it felt.

The English papers were readily available but I ignored them, just like I avoided English people. Even sight-seeing was off on Míkonos. There are some sights to savour, the gay universe at its preening exhibitionist, narcissistic best... or at its worst.

What would get you arrested in Britain seemed mandatory here. Lots of E, but I was a hot-house of pharmaceuticals already. One day, lying on the beach, a shadow fell across me. I opened my toasted lids to see Bob above me.

I said, 'Bob.'

'Jeez mate, yer burning up there. I brought you a cold one.'

I sat up and took it... gulped it down.

He nodded, said, 'Hits the spot, eh?'

'Yeah, that it does.'

He'd a good colour too. Dressed only in bermudas, he'd a beer-gut and a body that had taken some action for fifty years at least. He said, 'Yer a puzzle you are mate... you come to where it's all happening and live like a monk. Unless you have some floozy stashed in yer room. That it?'

'Naw, no floozy.'

'Well, you're not queer. Me 'n' Rodney, we can spot a nancy right off... So, were you misinformed? Maybe you heard Míkonos was the place for quietness?'

I smiled, said, 'What do you care Bob, eh? What's it to you? Thanks for the drink but it bought you civility not information.'

He spread his hands in a calming fashion, 'Whoa... back off, Tony. Me 'n' Rodney wanted to ask you to dinner... All right? A bit of a nosh-up with London boys only... okay?'

It was the last thing I wanted.

I said, 'Love to. What time?'

'Round nine – see you at the caff where we met, all right... ?'

24

Cats.

There are more of them than there are Germans in Greece. I was at a taverna with the boys and a plague of cats milled beneath the table.

Bob said, 'I'll order for us all... okay?'

'Sure.'

Even the waiter was gorgeous. It's an island where the mediocre is glaringly exposed. If you're ugly, go to Corfu, they expect it. Bob ordered:

Fava
Revitloiceftedes
Spanako rizzo
Tzazitei
Sheftalia
Melitz zanos

I figured he was:

a. Chancing his arm
b. Naming Greek footballers
c. Raving.

I asked shrewdly, 'Do you speak Greek?'

'Listened to cassettes for the past six months. I'm not always sure what I'm saying but it seems like it's what I would want. You've got to let a bit of flexibility float, plus it's kinda exciting.'

'Exciting?'

'Sure, you dunno, did you ask for chips or a wank?'

Is there a reply to this in any language? The waiter came scuttling with two bottles of Domestica, plonked them down.

Bob shouted, 'Yo' Costa, what cha fink yer doing with that shite... eh?'

Looked all right to me. It was yellowish and in a bottle and had a Greek name.

I said, 'Looks all right to me.'

'It's tourist wine. The Greeks wouldn't piss with it. Costa take this shite away, bring us some Aspro Krassi.' And he added, 'Mallakas'

Before I could ask, he said, 'Means wanker. They use it as a term of affection, or it's reach for your weapon time.'

A cat entwined itself round Bob's leg. He said:

'The thing with cats is... you can't train them not to kill cos it's what they do – it's who they are. You can train them not to kill in front of you and that's the best you can expect.'

Jeez, I thought, that's deep and said, 'Jeez, that's deep.'

'Naw, just a law of nature.'

Rodney was chain-chugging bottles of Amstel beer. I don't think I'd heard him speak.

I asked, 'Yer mate, he doesn't say a lot.'

'Not his thing... he likes to stay half-pissed, be mostly out of the game.'

'Tell you what, he's succeeding.'

The food came, the wine in tin beakers. It looked worse than the other stuff.

Bob said as he forked through a dish, 'This here is *Saganaki* which is like fried cheese, okay? Or hey, have some *papoutsaki*. They're aubergine halves stuffed with cheese and mincemeat.'

'I'd rather eat it than pronounce it.' He laughed.

I half turned my head and saw Roz walk towards me. The glass of wine fell outa my hand and my heart rocketed in my chest. As she drew nearer, the moment passed and I realised it wasn't her. Not even vaguely similar, though she was certainly an ugly cow too.

The information didn't filter through to my system and a tremor kicked my whole body.

Bob cried, 'Jeez son, are you all right? Don't get a coronary before I get me dessert.'

He put his hand on my shoulder, squeezed it... shouted to the waiter.'

'Get some *metaxa* over here.'

I forced myself to focus and gradually came back on line, said, 'I'm okay... guess it's this bloody flu.'

'It's the chick-peas do you in every time... you looked like you saw a ghost.'

'It's nothing, don't mean nothing... drive on.'

Rodney had been galvanised by my performance and began to intone in a sports commentator style:

'Mike Slater hooked in the second over, got a top edge and was caught by Graham Gooch. The Aussies were nine for one. England has squeezed another 27 runs out of their last three wickets. Fraser scored 28 off 29 balls, only one short of his highest test score...'

They he guzzled half an Amstel, sank back in his chair.

I said:

'Fuck, I thought he was a Crystal Palace supporter!'

'He is, but he does love his cricket.'

I stood up, if shakily, said, 'I think I'll call it a night.'

'Call it whatever you like, mate, I'll walk back with you.'

'No need... truly... thanks for the Greek lesson.'

Bob gave me the oddest look, said:

'Life is full of significant meetings. Only in hindsight or Hind Street do we realise what they meant. When you get time, remember the lesson of the cats... that's the important bit... you take care, mate. I enjoyed yer company.'

I felt too woozy to dwell on any of it. Figured I'd ask him next time. All I wanted to do was curl up under my sheets. If I'd known I'd never see them again, would I have behaved any differently? I like to think I'd at least have paid for the meal. They must have gone next morning, cos I searched in vain. A nagging suspicion that it had been a massive hallucination added to my pervading awfulness.

With them gone, Míkonos lost its appeal and I decided to give island-hopping a go. For the next two weeks, I blitzed across Greece...

… on boats
off boats
in bed
feverish
sun-bathing
pilling.

Went to Rhodes and was assaulted by waves of blonde hordes. The Scandinavians in all their pinched glory. Took a day trip to Turkey and that truly was hallucinatory. Bought two carpets and left them on the boat.

I was a deep mahogany brown colour, a whole lot slimmer and with the wire rimmed frames, looked like Ghandi after a bad night out.

I woke one morning in Kos to feel something on the side of my neck, wondering if Transylvania had moved and I'd been vampirised.

Stumbled out of bed and checked the mirror. Two lumps there and I swear I went ashen behind my tan. I knew what those were…

Sarcomas.

The advance guard of a death warrant.

Back in Athens, I laid out a minor ransom for the undivided attention of a Kolonaki doctor. Got the tests done and the results were peppered with him tut-tutting:

'Highly irregular, not my usual practice.'

I paid through the teeth.

Got the verdict I'd already known.

HIV positive with strong indication of the full-blown within a year.

Maybe less.

As I walked out into the sun of Kolonaki Square, in front of the British Council, with orange trees all round, I understood the meaning of Dead Man Walking.

It's all over, save the dying.

I'd also learnt that steroids hide the effects of the disease. Made you look good, too. Course the downside was moments of pure madness.

Well, I'd just add them to my baggage and let them stand in line for their shout at emergence.

Business as usual.

Booked a British Airways flight to London, a first class seat. I'd a day to wait so I went out to Glyfada to have a look at where Christina Onassis lived. Lay on the beach and listened to Lorena McKennit on the Walkman. Once, hearing the piece, 'The Lighting of the Lamps' would have me pine for a balcony in Marrakesh. But not – no how no more. Stayed on the beach 'til evening.

A British couple next to me said:

'Be careful of the ultra violet, you could get a melanoma.'

I said, 'Naw, I'm immune.'

And heard the husband mutter, 'Must be a Paddy.'

I should have said:

'Yeah, but a Paddy on steroids. Wanna fuck with that, Messrs United Kingdom?'

But that's how it goes. The lines always come too late. Just ask Neil Kinnock.

25

London was dark and pissing outa the heavens. As if I gave a fuck...

As I waited for my bag, a porter said, 'Brilliant tan.'

'Yeah.'

'Pity they fade, eh?'

'Not this one, I'm taking it with me.'

And left him to it. Now he'd really have a reason for scratching his arse.

Nolan said, 'Blimey, I thought I was being mugged by an extra from *Baywatch*.'

I'd watched his house all afternoon, saw him come home, then a little later, two women call and his wife leaves with them. Jackpot night at the bingo. I'd gone in through the back, something I was getting good at. Too late, alas, for a career change.

He was watching *Eastenders*. His shoes off and his feet resting on a pillow. Dressed in a shirt, braces and the trousers of that blue suit – the copper at ease.

I shoved the Browning in his ear, said:

'Young lad I knew hoped to audition for that.'

He half turned, saw who it was, did a double-take, then

made the *Baywatch* crack. I moved round front, adjusting the barrel to fit on his forehead, slid the catch, and as he heard the snap, sweat coated his face.

But he kept his voice steady, said:

'I thought they done you too.'

'Who's they?'

'Whoever did Reed with the blow-torches.'

Oh God! It must have shown on my face, cos he said, 'You didn't know! While you was sunning yerself, they was barbecuing yer mate.'

I whipped the gun back, then used it to break his nose.

He roared:

'Oh fucking hell... ah yah bastard.'

A trickle of blood fell on his shirt and he moved his sleeve to dab it.

I said, 'Leave it. As the Rolling Stones put it, "Let it Bleed".'

He tried to gather himself. Not easy with a recently broken nose but he was a feisty fucker.

He said:

'Yer a sick bastard.'

'Indeed I am... now here's the deal: I came to shoot you in the balls...' Let him digest that, then continued, 'But if you tell me what I need to know... maybe I won't.'

'Shoot a copper... I don't think so.'

I shot him in the hand, said:

'Think again... you're not a copper, you're a piece of shit. Now, do I have yer undivided attention?'

He nodded.

'Okay, tell me what's been happening?'

Between groans, he spat out that Leon's club had been blown to smithereens, taking Leon, his Minder and half of Electric Avenue, including Jimmy's Autos, with it. Reed's body had been dumped outside my home.

I considered all this, then asked, 'You said blow-torches?'

'Yeah.'

'Only one person we know who favours them.'

'Yeah, sending a message I'd say... You were bloody daft to come back.'

I moved away from him, said:

'No doubt I could ask you to keep shtoom – you'd probably even give me yer word, wouldn't yah?'

He was curled up on the couch, cradling his shattered hand. I'm not even sure he heard me.

I thought , Maybe I could risk it, just leave him.

I was at the door, about to go, when I added:

'On the other hand…'

I noticed *Eastenders* had finished.

HACK-MAN

26

Jack wouldn't be so easy to sneak up on, so I began to follow him… discreetly, carefully, religiously.

The thug duo went everywhere with him. In the evenings, once he was home, I went back to my hotel, watched TV.

As usual, repeats were the order of the day. Saw all the *Godfather I* and *II*. Even toyed with the idea of doing an Al Pacino. Meet Jack in a restaurant, have the gun stashed in the toilet.

Sure.

He'd probably seen the movie and stash my hands in the toilet. I thought of Reed all the time. The other deaths I'd blanked. Could go whole chunks of activity without them obtruding. But Reed just was. I saw some of him in every black face I saw.

In prison you can smell a riot coming. The days before, it turns very quiet.

Reed said:

'Okay, here's the deal – there's three stages involved with heavy duty rioting…

1. The Riot proper
2. The Reclaiming
3. The Reprisals…

…What we do is, we stay in this cell, we don't come out for nothin' or nobody. You hear me now?'

I heard him then, I hear him now.

It was one of the very few times he'd spoken in my accent. That got my attention most. When the riot came it was like opening a back door to hell. Course all the righteous dudes, they went after the nonces, the sex-offenders on Rule 43.

Hung them from the landings. The papers don't cover that.

Then they came for us with threats, bribes, hoses, and even fire. But Reed was a veteran and we came through.

After, he said:

'Dee worst shee-hit bro', dat be to die alone.'

I looked like I was going to let that happen. Put it on the rap-sheet of the damned. How could I have believed he'd leave London? A hundred times he'd said:

'Brixton be dee blues – dee blues be mo hearts beat.'

Once, to pass an evening, Reed and I went to an AA meeting in the nick. Got you outcha cell for an hour. You get biscuits, tea and free tobacco.

What I remember is the guy saying, 'When I'm uncertain, confused, dunno what to do, I up my meetings.'

So I upped my surveillance – it paid dividends.

Jack was down to one thug indoors. Each evening at seven, thug Number One accompanied him inside, Number Two drove off in the Audi.

I checked, rechecked to be certain this was the usual routine. It was.

Afternoons, I'd take an hour off, go roast on a sunbed. Brown to brownest. Now I resembled George Hamilton playing the part of a skinhead on the skids. The wire-rimmed glasses had an astounding effect. Made me appear intense and I was sure working on it.

Before, I'd hear someone say, 'I'm working on my tan,' I'd think, Nice work if you can get it.

I was getting close.

Them steroids make you want to kick ass… any ass. Kick, anyway.

Two-thirty in the morning.
They call it the dying time. I could go with that. Drove up there at a leisurely pace, I didn't want to be pulled over then. Dulwich isn't exactly where it's happening at the best of occasions; that hour, it's scarce-city.

Parked the car and was careful not to bang the doors. I was wearing a black tracksuit, black trainers. Jogged up to the house. I couldn't see any sign of activity. Went round the back and forced a ground-floor window, using a suction pad so as to hold the broken glass intact. I saw that in a movie and, I can testify, it works. Then I was able to open the full window and climb on in.

Among the scenarios I'd considered for Jack was something from one of his favourite actor's movies. For example, I'd toyed with *French Connection II*: pumping him full of heroin over a few days. Scratched that.

Stood rock-still in the kitchen as the sound of many voices carried.

'Jesus!' I said.

How wrong could I have got it... party night or what? Turned back to the window when the sound changed and I realised it was a video. Big breath of relief.

Tip-toed out and peeked in the living room. Jack was not only watching *Bonnie and Clyde* but talking back to the movie. Sounded like he knew it by heart. I reached in my waist-band for the Glock, but went for the Browning instead.

Two, three steps and wallop!

Jack slumped in the chair. I glanced at the screen, Gene was blinded and howling like a pig.

I said, 'Figures.'

And let him howl.

Went in search of Thug Number One. He was snoring like a horse in the upstairs bedroom. Prodded him gently awake and said, 'Don't ever interrupt me,' and coshed him with the Browning. I used the sheets as rope and packed his own socks into his mouth.

Bundled him into the closet, said, 'Homophobic that!'

I was sweating freely and reckoned I'd time to take a shower. Did that and used a variety of deodorants to freshen up, muttering, 'Some men can't help acting on impulse.'

Yeah.

Didn't re-dress but had a look round the house, enjoying the freedom being naked brings. Opened a door, hit the light, said:

'Holy Shit!'

It was a shrine to Roz. Framed pictures everywhere, close to a hundred, I'd guess. Centrepiece was a life-sized portrait that took up most of the wall, with bracket lights for emphasis. Looked as if she was coming right at you. A spooky feeling.

I said:

'You were a bad bitch then and you ain't improved.'

Closed the door on her.

Time for Jacko.

When he came round, he was tied, naked, to a kitchen chair. I was still in the buff and lounging on the sofa. A gag prevented any screaming. I'm real intolerant of it. His eyes bulged.

I said:

'I've got to hand it to you, fellah. Even unconscious, you're a definite nine.'

Sounds came from the gag, his body contorted in ferocious effort.

Continued... 'Yup, don't be shy, we did exchange body fluids. You probably don't remember when we met, one of the karaoke numbers was Hot Chocolate's "It Started With A Kiss". How's that for irony, eh?

'Oh yeah, I've just been tested and, alas, HIV positive – the middle-class disease. See those suckers on my neck, they're sarcomas. But no doubt you'll get to learn all this good shit for yerself. I'm going to split and...

'What can I say? Keep it buttoned, guy.'

ONE
WEEK
LATER

...

27

I'd planned on stopping the lithium.
Ride the mania high for the last time, then eat the Glock.
Then the slide began.

But, I'm curious as to how Jack will jump. Can he find a line of Gene's to cover this action?

That's gotta be interesting. Timothy Leary's final words were:

'Why not?'

Yeah. They fit.

BLOODLINES the cutting-edge crime and mystery imprint...

That Angel Look by Mike Ripley
"The outrageous, rip-roarious Mr Ripley is an abiding delight..."
– Colin Dexter

A chance encounter (in a pub, of course) lands street-wise, cab-driving Angel the ideal job as an all-purpose assistant to a trio of young and very sexy fashion designers.

But things are nowhere near as straightforward as they should be and it soon becomes apparent that no-one is telling the truth – least of all Angel! Double-cross turns to triple-cross and Angel finds himself set-up by friend and enemy alike. This time, Angel could really meet his match...

"I never read Ripley on trains, planes or buses. He makes me laugh and it annoys the other passengers." – Minette Walters.
ISBN 1 899344 23 3— £8

Fresh Blood II edited by Mike Ripley and Maxim Jakubowski
The first FRESH BLOOD anthology celebrated the "articulate and unpredictable voices" (*New York Times*) of the New Wave of British crime writers.

FRESH BLOOD II brings in a second wave of "crime writing with attitude" from some of the brightest talents of the '90s.

The mood is often dark, cruel and violent, sometimes funny, but always sharp.

There are few detectives – certainly none of the conventional kind – hardly any neat moral solutions, and not a single body in any library.

What you get are murderers, victims, thieves, con-men, gamblers, adulterers and contract killers.

Original stories, with introductions, from the authors, from the cream of British crime writers:

John Baker • Christopher Brookmyre • Ken Bruen • Carol Anne Davis Christine Green • Lauren Henderson • Charles Higson • Maxim Jakubowski • Phil Lovesey • Mike Ripley • Mary Scott • Iain Sinclair John Tilsley • John Williams • RD Wingfield
ISBN 1 899344 20 9— £8

BLOODLINES the cutting-edge crime and mystery imprint...

I Love The Sound of Breaking Glass by Paul Charles

First outing for Irish-born Detective Inspector Christy Kennedy whose beat is Camden Town, north London.

Peter O'Browne, managing director of Camden Town Records, is missing. Is his disappearance connected with a mysterious fire that ravages his north London home? And just who was using his credit card in darkest Dorset?

Detective Inspector Christy Kennedy and his team investigate, plumbing the hidden depths of London's music industry, turning up murder, chart-rigging scams, blackmail and worse. This is a detective story with a difference. Part whodunnit, part howdunnit and part love story, it features a unique method of murder, a plot with more twists and turns than the road from Kingsmarkham to St Mary Mead. Paul Charles is one of Europe's best known music promoters and agents. Here he reveals himself as master of the crime novel. ISBN 1 899344 16 0 – £7

"An intriguing glimpse of how the music business works... a smash hit!" –Press Association (*PA News*)

Shrouded by Carol Anne Davis

Douglas likes women — quiet women; the kind he deals with at the mortuary where he works.

Douglas meets Marjorie, unemployed, gaining weight and losing confidence. She talks and laughs a lot to cover up her shyness, but what Douglas really needs is a lover who'll stay still — deadly still.

Driven by lust and fear, Douglas finds a way to make girls remain excitingly silent and inert. But then he is forced to blank out the details of their unplanned deaths.

Shrouded is a powerful and accomplished début, tautly-plotted, dangerously erotic and vibrating with tension and suspense. It deserves to propel Carol Anne Davis to the forefront of young British writers. ISBN 1 899344 17 9 — £7

"Could well be the début of the year" –Janice Young, *Yorkshire Post*

Hellbent on Homicide by Gary Lovisi

"This isn't a first novel, this is a book written by a craftsman who learned his business from the masters, and in Hellbent On Homicide, *that education rings loud and long." –Eugene Izzi*

1962, a sweet, innocent time in America... after McCarthy, before Vietnam. A time of peace and trust, when girls hitch-hiked without a care. But for an ice-hearted killer, a time of easy pickings. Griff and Fats, Bay City's hardest homicide detectives, are pitted against a monster who tortures and kills, and time is running out...

"A wonderful throwback to the glory days of hardboiled American crime fiction." –Andrew Vachss

Brooklyn-based Gary Lovisi's powerhouse début novel is a major contribution to the hardboiled school, a roller-coaster of sex, violence and suspense, evocative of past masters like Jim Thompson, Carroll John Daly and Ross Macdonald. ISBN 1 899344 18 7 — £7

BLOODLINES the cutting-edge crime and mystery imprint...

Perhaps She'll Die! by John B Spencer

Giles could never say 'no' to a woman... any woman. But when he tangled with Celeste, he made a mistake... A bad mistake.

Celeste was married to Harry, and Harry walked a dark side of the street that Giles – with his comfortable lifestyle and fashionable media job – could only imagine in his worst nightmares. And when Harry got involved in nightmares, people had a habit of getting hurt.

Set against the boom and gloom of eighties Britain, *Perhaps She'll Die!* is classic *noir* with a centre as hard as toughened diamond.

ISBN 1 899344 14 4 — £5.99

Smalltime by Jerry Raine

Smalltime is a taut, psychological crime thriller, set among the seedy world of petty criminals and no-hopers. In this remarkable début, Jerry Raine shows just how easily curiosity can turn into fear amid the horrors, despair and despondency of life lived a little too near the edge.

"Jerry Raine's *Smalltime* carries the authentic whiff of sleazy nineties Britain. He vividly captures the world of stunted ambitions and their evil consequences."— Simon Brett

"The first British contemporary crime novel featuring an underclass which no one wants. Absolutely authentic and quite possibly important."– Philip Oakes, *Literary Review*

ISBN 1 899344 13 6 — £5.99

Fresh Blood edited by Mike Ripley & Maxim Jakubowski

"Move over Agatha Christie and tell Sherlock the News!" This landmark anthology features the cream of the British New Wave of crime writers: John Harvey, Mark Timlin, Chaz Brenchley, Russell James, Stella Duffy, Ian Rankin, Nicholas Blincoe, Joe Canzius, Denise Danks, John B Spencer, Graeme Gordon, the two editors, and a previously unpublished extract from the late Derek Raymond. Includes an introduction from each author explaining their views on crime fiction in the '90s and a comprehensive foreword on the genre from Angel-creator, Mike Ripley.

ISBN 1 899344 03 9 — £6.99

Quake City by John B Spencer

The third novel to feature Charley Case, the hard-boiled investigator of the future. But of a future that follows the 'Big One of Ninety-Seven' – the quake that literally rips California apart and makes LA an Island.

"Classic Chandleresque private eye tale, jazzed up by being set in the future... but some things never change – PI Charley Case still has trouble with women and a trusty bottle of bourbon is always at hand. An entertaining addition to the private eye canon."

— John Williams, *Mail on Sunday*

ISBN 1 899344 02 0 — £5.99

The Do-Not Press
Fiercely Independent Publishing

Keep in touch with what's happening at the cutting edge of independent British publishing.

Join The Do-Not Press Information Service and receive advance information of all our new titles, as well as news of events and launches in your area, and the occasional free gift and special offer.

Simply send your name and address to:
The Do-Not Press (Dept. HB)
PO Box 4215
London
SE23 2QD

There is no obligation to purchase and no salesman will call.

CHARLIE BYRNE
THE BOOK SHOP - GALWAY
05-05
€ 6·00